PANDORA'S BOX

PANDORA'S BOX

E. C. TUBB

WILDSIDE PRESS

OPENING PANDORA'S BOX

BY PHILIP HARBOTTLE

The decade following the Second World War changed the face of fiction publishing in the United Kingdom. During 1945-55, there was a veritable explosion in the number of SF novels and magazines being published. Post-war paper rationing and austerity measures meant that most of these publications were cheaply produced. Basing their opinions on appearances, SF historians and academics have virtually ignored the original books published during this period.

The first non-fiction book to treat the period in any depth was my own first book, *The Multi-Man* (1968), a bio-bibliographic study of John Russell Fearn. In it, I identified the many firms springing up as "mushroom" publishers, a term which has since become the accepted soubriquet for genre publishing in post-war Britain. Since then, I have published further books, including *British SF Paperbacks and Magazines 1949-56* (1994) and *Vultures of the Void: The Legacy* (2011). These books revealed that mixed in with the hackneyed rubbish of the fly-by-night publishers, were some highly collectable gems—the early works of talented writers whose only outlets were the mushroom publishers. And at the forefront of this small group of talented British writers was Edwin Charles Tubb.

Tubb's first short story, "No Short Cuts," was published in the Summer 1951 issue of *New Worlds* magazine. Tubb recalled how, as a young would-be novelist, he broke into the pocket book market: "I used to go to a pub with writers and fans, to the *White Horse* in London. One chap there, Dave Griffiths, told me: "Don't worry, boy, I'm a reader for Curtis Warren. You just let me have your novel. I'll put it in under my own name, they're bound to take it, and I'll pay you." Tubb wrote three novels which he passed to Griffiths, and they were duly published by Curtis Warren under their house names: *Saturn Patrol* as by King Lang (October 1951), *Planetfall* as by Gill Hunt (November 1951), and *Argentis* as by Brian Shaw (February 1952). "I actually got paid for the first one—still waiting for the other two!"

Although published under house names, they were immediately recognizable as the work of one talented author. They had action, colour and—a quality totally absent from contemporary novels—vivid *realism*. Amidst the clamour of strange machines and alien menaces, Tubb never forgot he was writing about human beings. His characters react in a logical and human manner to their surroundings and problems.

Before long, Tubb was being head-hunted by numerous other publishers. These included Hamilton & Co. (Stafford) Ltd., Scion Ltd., Milestone Ltd., and others. Now, his work was being published under his own name ("E.C. Tubb") or a personal pseudonym of his own choosing. In an interview with me in 1970 (printed in full in *Vultures of the Void: The Legacy*) Tubb was very frank about his earliest work. He pointed out that the mushroom publishers had a production schedule to maintain, and their habit of using their own house names "behind which the author lost both identity and responsibility" created a situation which "encouraged carelessness in writing and laid the emphasis on speed of production rather than quality."

By 1954, however, Tubb had thoroughly learned his craft, and his publishers, anxious to retain him, improved their terms. His first novel with Curtis Warren had earned just £27—for all rights. This had increased to £56, for English rights only. "By this time," Tubb recalls, "I was consciously trying to write the best material I could within the limits of the medium. The demand was always for fast, quick entertaining action—in fact the mixture as before—but now it could be smoother, with greater attention paid to detail and characterization."

Now firmly established as a full-time writer, Tubb was at the peak of production, writing for every one of Britain's SF magazines, and his novels were being issued from several publishers simultaneously. *Pandora's Box* (under the working title of *Greed*) was written in May 1954, and was quickly followed by a shorter novel, *The Temple of Dra Vheera* (at only 30,000 words it was intended for C.A. Pearson's "Tit-Bits" novella series). Married with a family, Tubb was about to move into a larger house. But then came a sudden collapse of the market for paperback novels!

Tubb recalled its effects on him: "For fear of being prosecuted for selling obscene material, the sellers simply refused to accept anything from these publishers. So your gangsters and your SF and westerns wouldn't sell: end of boom! And that hit me very hard at the time, because I'd just bought a house. I was left with a mortgage and no job and no (book) publishers, which meant I had to scurry around like the proverbial blue-arsed fly to get a job and keep the wolf from the door."

In fact, Tubb continued to write for the still-viable UK magazine market, and he also began to sell to the American SF magazines. It would be in America that he would later gain his greatest success as a novelist, with his "Dumarest" series. But in the meantime, what had become of his two unpublished novels written for the mushroom publishers?

Attending a British science fiction convention not long afterwards, Tubb was introduced to Anna Steul, a German literary agent. She told him of an emerging European market, where a number of British 1950s SF paperbacks were beginning to enjoy a new lease on life in translation. John Russell Fearn's "Vargo Statten" novels had started the trend, appearing regularly in France since 1952. The success of "Vargo Statten" had opened the door for E. C. Tubb, who would go on to blaze an even brighter trail across Europe.

Steul thereafter acted as Tubb's German agent, and he gave her his typescripts of both unpublished novels. *Greed* soon found a German publisher, retitled as *The Spore Menace*, but *The Temple of Dra Vheera*, due to its awkward short-novella length, did not, and it was eventually lost. However, many of Tubb's already-published novels were reprinted in German translations, and Tubb went on to appear in other European countries. Nearly all of his many Scion, Panther, Curtis, and Milestone novels saw one or more translations, long after their original English publishers disappeared. But for English and American readers, it seemed that they were destined never to see—or even know about—Tubb's two "lost" novels. But fate was ready to take a hand…

In the 1970s—probably stimulated by the success of the *Star Wars* movies—there was another surge of interest amongst European publishers for the old-style adventure novels of the 1950s, particularly in Italy. As the agent for John Russell Fearn's widow, I was contacted by Italian editors and publishers who still remembered the success of the "Vargo Statten" novels 20 years earlier. I was asked to supply copies of his novels for new translations. One of the more enterprising Italian editors—Antonio Bellomi of Milan—learned of my enthusiasm for Tubb's work. He enquired through me if copies of Tubb's early novels were available, and I was pleased to assist. I arranged for the first Italian editions of *Alien Life, World at Bay* and *Atom-War on Mars.* I mentioned to Tubb that I was also selling some of Fearn's unpublished novels, such was his posthumous popularity. Did *he*, I wondered, have any unpublished older material? It was then that he told me of the existence of his two unpublished novels, and after an intensive search, he managed to locate his only surviving carbon copies, which he loaned me.

I adjudged the novels to be highly suitable and photocopied them with the intention of sending them to Italy. But just at that moment, Tubb's "Dumarest" series was optioned by a prestigious Italian publisher, Mondadori. At the request of Tubb's then-agent, Les Flood, the novels were never sent because their appearance as new works from smaller publishers might have undermined his negotiations to place Dumarest in the higher paying market.

They remained in limbo over the next two decades. Then, enter Gary Lovisi, head of the Gryphon Publications small press in New York. Gary had been running articles by me on the 1950s

British SF scene in his magazine *Paperback Parade*. After I had written about them in his magazine, Gary decided that it would be a good idea to reprint the set of four John Russell Fearn novels chronicling the Burroughs-like adventures of his hero Clayton Drew, an Earthman who became Emperor of Mars. These were duly published by Gryphon in August 1995, and prompted me to visit Gary in New York when I was in the U.S.A. on holiday with my daughter. I passed copies of the unpublished Tubb novels to Gary and commended them as deserving of publication. He agreed, and thanks to his perspicacity and the kind cooperation of Ted Tubb, who was then representing himself following the retirement of his agent, both books were published in English for the first time. I retitled *The Spore Menace* as *Pandora's Box*.

And now *Pandora's Box* is appearing as part of Wildside's ambitious Tubb rediscovery series. The novel is no hoary relic of a bygone era. As previously noted, by 1954 Tubb had begun to develop the style and themes which he was later to perfect into a unique blend of vigorous action and human insight, exemplified in his famous "Dumarest of Terra" series.

Many of the ideas in this novel are seminal, even prophetic. Tubb was one of the very first SF writers to realize the potential danger to Earth from alien organisms. With the establishment of interplanetary contacts and space travel on a commercial basis, it is logical and necessary that strict quarantine and Customs Controls are brought into play and ruthlessly enforced. This has been universally overlooked by other writers. And whilst many of Tubb's contemporaries in the 1950s saw the Earth of the future as a bland semi-utopia, Tubb appreciated that whilst technology may change, Man's nature remains the same. *Pandora's Box* spins a fascinating tale based on that most basic human emotion—*greed*! Extrapolated into an interplanetary setting, it makes for a fine novel.

CHAPTER 1

Trouble came with the first delivery. Nothing much, a normal thing, just the warning hum of the buzzer and the rattle of the letter flap as a few, neatly folded sheets of paper slid into the container. But an explosion couldn't have had more effect.

John Weston stood at the door, riffling the letters, frowning a little as he read the return addresses. Slowly he walked back towards the breakfast table shoved against the wall of one room of the tiny two-roomed apartment.

"Mail, John?"

"Yes."

"Finish your breakfast, dear. It will get cold." His wife, a synthetic blonde with puffed eyes and traces of old makeup still visible on her petulant features, tried to smile. She didn't make a good job of it.

"No thanks." He pushed away the half-empty plate of lukewarm, yeast-vat cereal and thumbed open one of the letters.

"Lucy Margroves is going to Earth next week." Madge lit a cigarette and blew a streamer of blue smoke across the littered table. "On vacation to the North Polar Resort. When can we go, John?"

"I don't know." He didn't look at her as he opened the rest of the letters. "It costs money to go to Earth and more money to stay at swank holiday resorts. We can't afford it, Madge, you know that." He touched the opened letters. "Why did you do it?"

"Do?" She dragged nervously at her cigarette. "Do what?"

"You know what I'm talking about." He riffled the letters. "All these bills."

"So I bought a few things. What of it?"

"What of it?" He sighed as he looked at her, seeing her perhaps for the first time as she really was. He thinned his lips at the hardness of her eyes, her skin, a little riddled now without the normal heavy makeup, the downward curve of the lips and the faint lines digging their way from nose to mouth. "If you don't know," he said quietly, "I can't tell you."

"Are you complaining again?" Anger made her voice harsh. "What am I supposed to do, just sit in this box and twiddle my thumbs?"

"You could be reasonable." He picked up the bills. "Fresh food, two hundred and fifty credits. Liquor, five seventy. Clothes, three ninety. Cosmetics, two twenty. Television, one ninety. Damn it, woman, did you just sit here staring at the television and drinking yourself sick all day? And the fresh food; what's the matter with the Dome rations?" He slammed the bills down on the table. "It's got to stop, Madge, and stop for good."

"Has it?" She glared at him through the smoke from her cigarette. "I'm human, John, or have you forgotten? A girl like me needs nice things and I've just got to have them." Abruptly she seemed to lose her anger. Rising, she stepped to his side and ran her fingers through his hair. "Don't you like to see me look nice, John? Do you want to see me miserable because you aren't happy?" She kissed the top of his head. "Stop worrying, you old silly. What's a few credits more or less?"

"A damn lot," he said tightly. "I'm just not earning that sort of money."

"Money!" She spun away from him, glaring with naked hate. "You're always whining about money! I've got a right to decent things. I've got to have fresh food. Those stinking rations turn my stomach. And I've got a right to nice clothes and perfume. Every girl has. It isn't fair to ask me to give up everything just because..."

"Because I cracked up and had to take this job on the Moon?" John shrugged. "Perhaps you're right. In the old days it was easy. A space pilot earns good money, and you could spend it as you wanted. But things are different now, Madge. You've got to realise that."

"You think I don't?" She sat down again, her mouth a bitter line. "Stuck up here in the Dome with you beating your brains out, acting like a third-rate customs inspector when you should be getting big money piloting the interplanetary liners. Sitting in this dump, shift after shift, with nothing to do but look at the relayed television shows. Trying to be pleasant to women who don't know the first thing about a decent social life. Scrimping and doing without, worrying, when I do have a few small pleasures, you begrudge them."

"Five hundred seventy credits for liquor isn't what I'd call simple pleasure."

"So I had a few friends in for a drink. So what?"

"So you've got to cut it out." John rose to his feet. "I'm not joking, Madge. You've got to get rid of the old ideas and get some sense. I'm not earning a fifth of what I used to get, and the way things are, I'm lucky to be working at all. Other women manage to live on Dome rations and enjoy themselves without running up big bills for liquor and fresh food. You've got to do the same."

"I can't, John. I won't. It isn't fair to ask me." She caught his arm. "I followed you, didn't I? I came up here with you to share your life here at Luna Station, gave up all my friends, my career, everything which made life worth living."

"Your career?" He stared down at her distorted features. "You mean those commercials you used to show a leg in? The girlie shows and stocking ads? Career?"

"You swine! You can talk like this now, but I remember the time when you wouldn't take no for an answer. I didn't chase you John. You chased me, and you just remember that!"

"Don't remind me," he said tiredly. "That was back in the good old days when I had money to burn, and you knew how to be nice. You've changed since then, Madge. Maybe we've both changed, I wouldn't know. But let's leave the past where it belongs, shall we?"

"You'd like to forget it, wouldn't you?" She didn't trouble to hide her sneer. "Just you remember that I'm the girl you married and I'm the girl you've got to support. And if you think that I'm going be satisfied with this doghouse, you want to think again!"

"You could get a job," he suggested. "We've no children, and there's nothing to stop you from working." He gripped her shoulder. "How about it, Madge? I could get you in at the inspection sheds and with what you'd earn we'd almost double my salary. Shall I ask at the office?"

"Work?" She laughed in his face. "You think I got married just to work? No, John. You're my meal ticket and I'm taking good care that you don't forget it. Now run along like a good boy or you'll be late for duty, and you can't afford to lose any time." She yawned. "I'm tired. I think I'll catch up on my beauty sleep. Don't slam the door when you go out."

"You bitch!" For a moment it seemed as if he would strike her and she cowered, one hand lifted as if to ward off a blow. Then he shrugged. "Remember what I said, Madge. No more bills."

"I'll watch it." She laughed, a brittle sound more of malice than humour. "My credit's good and my lawyer tells me that you can't cut if off. While you're my husband, you're responsible for my debts. But don't worry, John. I know just how far to go. I won't kill the goose which lays the golden eggs."

He stared at her, something of his old self returning to heat his eyes with brown fire, and his slender figure trembled as he fought the desire to slap her sneering face. He resisted it. She was his wife, for better or worse. The abrupt transition from being the wife of a well-paid space pilot who was only home on infrequent leaves to being the wife of a low-paid customs inspector and having to live in the cramped quarters of Tycho Station must have been a shock. She was no longer at her first youth, hadn't been when he married her, but had managed to hide her true age with skilfully applied cosmetics.

Now she couldn't afford to leave him, couldn't run the risk of being left on the shelf with no one to provide bed and board and shelter her from the commercial rat-race back on Earth. And the way the laws were framed, he couldn't divorce her without sacrificing half of his income in alimony.

He was well and truly caught.

Tired, he left the apartment, shrugging his uniform about his shoulders as he walked slowly down the stairs and away from the building. Outside, he glanced up at the huge transparent dome protecting the station from the void and stared with nostalgic longing at the great ball of Earth, shining green and blue, brown and fleecy white against the black, star-shot background of space. It was night on the Moon, the long, fourteen-day night, and there was no sun-glare to detract from the limpid beauty of the Mother World. He stood looking at it, remembering the green fields and warm rain, the rippling brooks and the powerful surge of the restless seas, the feel of summer's sunshine and the clean, crisp, unbearable beauty of freshly fallen snow. Gone now. All gone, for, unless he could save enough to pay for passage back, he would be exiled here until he died.

. And saving wasn't easy. A single man might just be able to do it. A single man could live in bachelor quarters, eat at the communal restaurant, cut out all luxuries and skimp to the bone. But a married man, one whose wife refused to work, found it impossible. And Madge refused even to try. He pursed his lips as he thought about it, recalling the hard lines of her aging features, the petulance of her down-curved mouth and the selfish obstinacy which made her refuse to admit facts and to pledge his credit, wasting his financial reserve on luxury goods and expensive importations.

Dully he wondered what their life would be when she had finally exhausted his reserves and they had to live wholly on his salary. A woman brushed past him, smiling with open friendliness and recognised the wife of one of the spaceport engineers.

"Going on duty, John?"

"Yes, Seela. And you?"

"It's time for my shift at the yeast vats." She wrinkled her nose with mock disdain. "Sometimes I wonder how I ever manage to eat the stuff after working with it all day. Still, I mustn't grumble. The pay's useful and it won't be forever."

"How's that, Seela? Are you going back home soon?"

"Perhaps." She smiled with a warm cheerfulness which filled him with a sick envy of her engineer husband. "It's all a deep secret as yet, and you must promise not to tell a soul, but we may be leaving within the month."

"For Earth?"

"Where else?"

"But..."

"My father's sent for us. He's managed to buy a small farm. We sent him the money, of course, and Sam is going to give up his engineering and turn into a dirt farmer." She hunched her shoulders in anticipation. "Just think of it, John! Growing real plants instead of messing about with yeast cultures. Feeling the soil on your hands and the sun on your face. No more canned air and cramped quarters. I could even have children, lots of children. I've always wanted kids." She saw his expression and paused. "Is anything wrong, John?"

"No, Seela. Nothing."

"I thought..." She shrugged. "How's Madge?"

"Well enough." He glanced at the chronometer strapped to his wrist. "I must hurry. If you will excuse me..." She nodded as he strode away, glad to hide his envious expression, fighting the frustration burning within him. Damn it! Why couldn't Madge be like that? But she wasn't, and there was nothing he could do about it. Maybe he had been a fool to marry in the first place, but money had been plentiful, the life glamourous and he had been fooled by superficial charm and calculated affection. Now it was over, and he had to be content with what was left.

It wasn't much.

A rocket ship, its exhaust a long, blue-white streak across the heavens, swung above the landing field and began to descend on its pencil of flame. Watching it, he felt his hands twitch as, in imagination, he grasped familiar controls, feeling again the throb and pulse of power as massed weight fought against the thrust of speeded ions, living for a moment the thrill and exultation of pitting human skill against the gravitational drag of a world.

He sighed, knowing that those days were over forever and that it was time he reported for duty. Quickly he weaved his way through the narrow lanes, passed the bleak walls of the refining and air-conditioning plants, skirted the yeast factory and crossed the open space before the transient hotel. A uniformed man nodded to him as he checked in at the customs sheds and his opposite number grunted as he turned from the wide, flat counter running across the entry section.

"It's all yours, John. Ship from Mars just coming in and special orders to watch for narcotics." He wiped a hand across his lips. "Hell, but I'm dry. Think I'll have me a couple before turning in. Be seeing you." John nodded and checked his section.

The work wasn't hard, but it wasn't easy. With some of the alien narcotics worth double their weight in refined uranium, with enthusiastic amateurs willing to pay through their noses for extra-Terrestrial seeds and spores, with the natural cussedness of the human race which made it a smart action to sneak curios and souvenirs through the clearing station and down to Earth, John had his work cut out. It was the terrible danger from blights and drugs, from seeds and spores which, while innocuous on their own worlds, could cause havoc with the life cycle of Terrestrial plant and animal life which had forced the establishment of Luna Station. Here, all cargoes bound for Earth were trans-shipped from the big interplanetary liners, passengers passed through the customs and health inspections, and the cleared goods and travellers rerouted by the stubby, short-shot rockets to the spaceports covering Earth.

He quickly checked his electronic instruments; the metal detector, which registered the amount of metal carried; the fluoroscope, an advanced form of X-ray, which could reveal small packages hidden beneath the skin; the weight scale, to check the incoming passengers against their transit cards. He looked up as the first passenger entered the shed.

It was a woman, a harmless-looking, motherly soul, and she carried a shapeless bag as she headed towards the wide counter. John smiled at her as she halted before him, deftly flicking his switches and glancing at the instruments. No metal, no hidden packages, no excess weight. That didn't mean anything. A smuggler would know of the electronic devices and guard against them.

His job depended more on psychology than anything else, and it rested with him whether or not he should order the woman stripped and searched in one of the cubicles.

"Anything to declare?"

"Don't be silly, young man. Do you take me for a smuggler?"

"Any seeds, plants, curios?" John didn't bother to answer her question.

"I must warn you that any concealment is punishable by imprisonment, a heavy fine, or both." He reached for her bag. "Open, please."

"This is ridiculous!" Anger drew in her cheeks and turned her mouth to a thin line of outraged dignity. "I'll have you know that I am the President of the Wives of Space and I expect due consideration from the servants of the public."

"Your bag." John pulled it towards him and opened the container. Articles spilled onto the counter, flimsy garments, notes, onion skin books, a photograph, a piece of rock and a transparent plastic vial of multi-coloured sand from the deserts of Mars. John stared at it, nodding as he saw the government seal denoting that it had been heat-sterilised, but passed it beneath the spectroscope to make sure. It showed the characteristic lines of heat-treatment and he returned it together with the other articles. He poised the lump of rock in his hand. "Did you collect this, madam?"

"Certainly I did. The prices the government store was asking for a bit of stone was simply ridiculous. Why, all I had to do was to walk out a little way and pick it up. It would have been criminal to pay what they were demanding."

"And yet you bought the sand?"

"Yes." She flushed a little but met his eyes. "I'm not wholly ignorant, young man. I have read of the danger. There could be spores, couldn't there?"

"That's right. Spores and maybe eggs, insect eggs." John shook his head as he looked at the rock. "I'm sorry, madam, but I will have to confiscate this."

"Ridiculous!"

"No, madam. Unless this material has been heat-treated, I cannot allow it to pass. Spores have been found embedded in rock, eggs, too. Sorry." He shrugged and dropped the stone into the disposal chute. Sealing her bag, he pushed it back across the counter and stamped his red seal on her transit card. "That is all, madam. You may pass on now."

"How dare you!" Red spots marred the smooth contours of her cheeks. "I'll complain about this! I'll have you discharged! I'll..."

"If you wish to complain, madam, the Superintendent is in that office." John pointed down the shed. "He will be happy to accommodate you. Now, if you will excuse me, please." He pressed the button unlocking the exit gate and rested his other hand on the electronic lock of the entry gate. "Hurry, please. There are other passengers waiting to be cleared."

She hesitated, biting at her thin lips. Then, with a snort of anger, picked up her bag and strode towards the Superintendent's office. John shrugged as he watched her go. The Super was a man trained in tact. He would smooth her down, promise to punish the offending officer, sympathise with her—then promptly forget all about it. John returned to his work.

A college girl came next, giggling but innocent. Cleared. Her friend, almost a carbon-copy of a famous television star, followed. Cleared. A businessman in a hurry. Cleared. A schoolteacher on her vacation. Confiscate two specimens. Cleared. A smooth-faced man with restless eyes and a sleek manner...

John flipped the switches and glanced down at his instrument. Nothing, but he hadn't expected any results. The small carryall showed nothing, not even the inevitable curio of the tourist, or the accumulated jumble of the constant traveller. The man appeared to be clean, too clean, but a tiny shred of suspicion nagged at John's mind. There was something, maybe the way the eyes shifted, or the tongue moistened the lips, or it may have been the too-easy manner, the too-soft hands. John didn't know, but he hesitated, his hand on the exit gate key, trying to place just what could be wrong.

"Hurry up, buster," snapped the man. "I want to snatch a drink before take-off."

"Going to Earth?"

"Can't you tell that from the transit card?" The man shifted and pushed against the bars of the exit gate. "Hurry, will you?"

"Turn out your pockets."

"What?" The man frowned, then shrugged. "Why not? You mind if I smoke?" He produced a cigar case and lit one of the fat brown cylinders. "I've been waiting for this ever since we left Mars."

John reached out and took the cigar case. He stared at the cylinders, tipped them out into his palm and hefted the case. He looked at the man.

"You fetch these all the way from Mars?"

"Yes."

"I see." John stepped back as his foot trod on a button. "All right, fellow. The guards will be here soon. Just take it easy until they arrive." He picked up a scalpel and deliberately slit one of the cigars along the smooth surface. The keen blade touched plastic and he snorted with contempt. "What is it? Happy Dust? Seeds? Spores or eggs?" He threw the cigars into a flat container and smiled as the man lunged at the metal bars hemming him in. He snarled as he pushed against them, lunging towards John as if to leap over the counter towards him, then halted at the sight of the high velocity pistol pointing at his stomach.

"Look," he gasped urgently. "Forget this. Ten thousand credits if you will let me through with the stuff."

"Forget it." John slipped the pistol into its holster as the guards arrived. He pressed the release button and the uniformed men snapped handcuffs around the man's wrists as they took him away. The guard leader sniffed at the opened cigar and stared at John.

"How did you suspect this one?"

"Simple. He fell down on two counts. No man would carry cigars across space, the freight rates are too high to carry something you can't use and which you can buy at either end. Also, he said the cigars were of Martian manufacture. They look it, all right, but he lit one and I know the difference between Havana leaf and the hydroponic stuff they use on Mars." He rolled the cigar with the tip of his finger. "You'll probably find narcotics. He offered me ten thousand to pass him through."

"I'll check on it." The guard officer stamped the report book and sealed the cigars in a plastic envelope. "Ten thousand, eh? The dope peddlers must be getting desperate." He nodded. "Good hunting."

John turned back to his work.

It took three hours to pass them all. Most caused no trouble. One flushed and admitted that he was carrying seeds for a friend who was interested in alien vegetation, a tourist who lost his nerve at the last moment. John destroyed the seeds, had the man stripped and searched, then read him a lecture and passed him through. The smuggler came last of all.

"Anything to declare?"

"No, and don't bother to read off the list, I've nothing at all."

"No?" John flipped his switches and glanced at the meters. He frowned, checking the weight against the transit card, then looked at the man. "There's a difference of three ounces. How do you account for it?"

"I don't."

"I see." John stared at the man, feeling the tug of suspicion but spotting nothing to be suspicious about. "Turn out your pockets."

He stared at the usual essentials carried: the identity card, a few personal papers, some paper money, transit card and a thin chronometer. The man didn't say anything, just stood waiting patiently while John examined his belongings.

"Have you any objection to being stripped and searched?"

"Have I any choice?" The man shrugged. "Go ahead, if it will make you happy." He waited calmly as John spoke into the hush-a-phone and walked with an attendant to the cubicle. John waited, resting his aching legs against the edge of the counter. He smiled as the attendant came out of the cubicle and nodded.

"You'll be getting a promotion if you keep this up, John. Two in one shipload. I've sent for the guards."

"Where did he keep it?"

"Stomach. I gave him the vomit-shot with a hand-hypo as you ordered and he brought it up like a hero. A plastic egg, probably with the same refraction density as normal flesh, and packed with narcotics. How did you spot it, John? This is the first time they've tried that one that I know of."

"I just guessed. I don't know how I know, but there was something wrong about him." John shook his head. "I can't explain it."

"I know how it is." The attendant nodded. "You took a chance, though. What if you'd been wrong?"

"I wasn't." John rested his aching head against the coolness of the wall as he watched the attendant walk back to the cubicle. If he'd been wrong, he would have had to face the Superintendent and a complaint charge of unorthodox behaviour. As he had guessed right, the machines would be altered to catch the new methods of the interplanetary smugglers.

He sighed and stopped thinking about it, resting until the next ship touched down and the routine would have to be gone through again.

He tried not to think of Madge.

CHAPTER TWO

Luna Station never slept. With a staggered twelve-hour working shift, there were always people going to or coming from their work and shops and taverns stayed open all around the clock. For once John was glad of it. He checked out with a head almost splitting with pain and a mouth which matched his eyes for aching discomfort. The yeast-vat culture food served at the customs shed cantina rested uneasily in his stomach and his nerves jumped and quivered from too much concentration and too much personal worry.

It had been a busy shift. First the Mars rocket, then a couple of freighters from Venus, with scowling, impatient crews eager to get going on their home leave. A small, express passenger/mail from the Jovian System and a heat-scarred hulk from Mercury. He closed his eyes as he stood outside the sheds, seeing again in imagination the long procession of faces, some defiant, some indifferent, a few scared without reason, and a few scared with good cause. Three smugglers had been caught and five people warned. An assortment of contraband had been confiscated and destroyed. A few enemies made and a half-dozen arrogant women smoothed down in the Super's office.

A busy shift.

He opened his eyes as he heard his name, and a small, expensively dressed man crossed over towards him. "Hello, John. Going on shift?"

"Just finished." John stared at him, not liking or disliking the small man. They had first met at a party, one of the desperate, intimate affairs Madge had started giving before he had insisted that they couldn't afford lavish hospitality. Most of the hangers-on had fallen away when he had cut off their supplies of free food and liquor, but the small man had stayed, and John suspected that he saw a little too much of Madge while he was busy at the sheds.

Not that he minded. Madge was too shrewd to give him the slight-est possible grounds for any divorce in which she would be the guilty, and therefore the losing party. Also, he had a sneaking idea that Phil was more interested in him than in Madge, in his job, that is, and sometimes he wondered why.

"Good." Phil smiled and glanced at the thick chronometer strapped to his wrist. "How about a drink?"

"No, thanks."

"Come on. Hell, man, you look as if you could do with one." Phil smiled again. "My treat. I had a lucky winner and I feel like celebrating."

For a moment John felt like refusing the obvious charity, then he shrugged. Phil had slopped enough of his liquor in the past, and he could afford it, which John couldn't. Also, he needed the offered drink. He followed the small man into a tavern.

"How's it going, John?" Phil put two tall glasses on the table and sat opposite the uniformed man. "Getting you down?"

"What makes you think that?"

"Your eyes, John, and your mouth. When you first came here you didn't look as you do now." Phil sipped at his drink. "There are signs of strain, tension, just as though there's something eat-ing your heart out. What's the matter, John? Want to get back into space?"

"Are you trying to be funny?" John gulped half his drink and felt the warm glow as the alcohol hit his stomach. "You know what happened to me. I cracked up, wrecked a ship on a bad land-ing and lost two lives and half the cargo. When you do things like that, they take your license away from you—for keeps."

"But it wasn't your fault, John. Didn't the medics..."

"Sure. I had swamp fever. We all did. And I had to bring her down alone. But I was the captain and the responsibility was mine." Liquor slopped as John drained the glass. "I could have thrown her into orbit, waited for a relief pilot to come out to bring her down. That's what I should have done and I know it."

"Swamp fever is a funny thing, John. It's like getting drunk: You aren't really responsible for what you do. They must have known that."

"Forget it."

"But I think you got a raw deal, John. It wasn't fair to ground you all because of one mistake."

"I said forget it!" John stared down at his trembling hands. "I don't want to talk about it. I don't even want to think about it."

"Sure, John. Sure." Phil snapped his fingers towards the waitress, a tall, thin, scarlet-haired girl with a deadpan expression and the blue tinge of malnutrition showing through her too-heavy makeup. "Have another drink." He gave the order and waited until the girl had set down the refilled glasses. "How's the finances?"

"What do you think?" John glowered at the small man over the rim of his glass.

Phil shrugged. "If you ask me, I'd say not too good." He hesitated. "Look, John, maybe it's none of my business, but if you're strapped and need a loan..."

"I'm not and I don't, but you're right about one thing."

"Yes?"

"It's none of your damn business!"

"Sure." Phil grinned with easy familiarity and slipped a bulging wallet from an inside pocket. "I'll just pay for the drinks and you can forget we ever met."

He opened the wallet and, despite himself, John felt a quick stab of envy at the sight of the thick sheaf of bills. He also felt a quick bit of shame. The man was only trying to be helpful, and in return he had been insulted. John smiled. "Sorry, I know that you mean well, but..."

"Forget it." Phil gestured towards the waitress. "Get some more drinks, miss, and keep the change."

Her eyes widened at the size of the note he tossed towards her, and her high heels drummed on the plasta-flooring as she ran to get the drinks.

Phil jerked his head towards where she stood. "I knew her when she first came up here. Married to a spacehand with one kid.

Her husband got caught in a blast. They couldn't even find his ashes. Now she's killing herself trying to scrape up the fare back home,"

He fell silent as she returned with the drinks and John squirmed as he saw the grateful expression in her eyes as she stared at Phil before leaving.

"You notice that blue tinge? Starvation. Living on the cheapest residues from the vats, half of it little better than poison. They let her work here now, but in a few months, when her health gives out..." He shrugged and John knew what he meant. There was no charity on the Moon. There couldn't be. To remain an efficient unit the station had room only for those who could afford to pay their way. If the woman lost her battle with her failing health, she would be pauperised, her money taken to pay for dome and air rent, her child sent to an institution on Earth, and she herself bonded to the yeast plant to work twelve hours a day for a nominal wage until she either bought her freedom or died. And very few were able to buy their freedom.

John felt his hands tighten around the glass as he thought of it. The same threat hung over everyone in the station. Everyone. And if Madge didn't get some sense and cut down her extravagances...

The thought of it made him sweat.

"You know," said Phil casually. "There might be a way to get a little extra money." He stared at John. "If you're interested, that is."

"Yes?" John forced himself to keep calm. He could guess what was coming, and he felt bitterness in the realisation that the small man had cultivated his friendship for but one reason. "What is it?" The answer surprised him.

"Gambling." Phil looked at his fingernails. "Ever wondered how I get a living, John?"

"Sometimes. Why?"

"I've got a friend, an engineer at the pits, and he tips me off just which rocket is going to win on the circuits. I place a thousand for him each time, and it's worth every credit of it." He looked at John. "If you're really up against it, and I think that you are, I might be able to help. The odds aren't too good, three, two, sometimes four to one. Sometimes it's even money, sometimes it's less than that but, with inside information, I get by." He looked at his fingernails again. "I know that officially you're not allowed to gamble, but if you feel like taking a chance..."

"Where will I place the bet?"

"I can fix that."

"And what about the other stuff? The inside information? Are you suggesting that I share it with you?"

"No." Phil smiled as if at an inward joke. "Not that, John. I trust you, but you might get careless. And another thing, I don't always get it until a few minutes before blast-off and there wouldn't be time to contact you." He shrugged. "If you want to take a chance and feel that you can trust me, I'll take your money and place it with my own. Maybe you'll win, maybe not. I can't promise, but personally I know what I'd do."

"Yes." John stared down at his drink and swallowed half of it down. "So I'm to give you my cash and then just cross my fingers." He laughed. "You know, I thought that you were about to proposition me. I'm glad that you didn't."

"Proposition?" Phil shrugged. "I know what you mean." He leaned forward. "What would you have done if I had?"

"Smashed your face in!" John finished his drink. "But you didn't, so let's forget it. How much do you want?"

"That's up to you, but remember, I can't guarantee that you will win."

"I'll give you a hundred for a starter." John rose to his feet. "I'll get it from the bank as we pass." He paused, biting his lip. "No. On second thought, that wouldn't be too wise. You're known around the station and people might get ideas. Call for it at the apartment when I'm on next shift. Madge will give it to you and you can tip me off when I win."

"If you win," reminded Phil. "There's nothing certain about it."

"The only thing certain at the moment," said John bleakly, "is that I'm on a sure loser. The quicker I get off, the better."

He didn't look at the waitress as he left the bar.

Madge was out when he got home, probably at one of her innumerable gossip sessions, or at a bar trying to find a listener for a private tale of self-imagined woe. John slammed the door of the empty apartment, took a quick spray-shower and gulped half a dozen B-right tablets. For a moment he toyed with the idea of going out trying to find her, then, as the soporific drugs took effect, tumbled into bed.

When he awoke she was still out but, from the empty cans and bottles in the living room, he guessed that she had returned for a meal or private drink session and had gone out again to the sweat baths. He tucked the money into an envelope, scrawled hasty instructions on the outside, and hurried to work. The tablets had given him a good night's rest and their compound of drugs had banished his depression and pains. The effect would pass, of course, it always did, and more of the insidious tablets would be needed but, in the meanwhile, he felt fine. He wasn't even annoyed with Madge. She had played this trick before, stopping out until he was worried sick about her, and then coming back full of affection and forgiveness.

The euphoria of the drugs was so strong that he passed the shift mentally counting up just how much he was going to win, and it wasn't until he was checking out that normal reason returned.

"Weston." A guard touched his shoulder. "The Super wants to see you."

"The Super?" John swallowed. "Why?"

"How should I know?" The guard shrugged. "Why don't you ask him yourself?"

The Superintendent was a sleek production of one of the best universities on Earth. A combination of smooth diplomacy and calculated brutality. A subtle mind coupled with a single-minded devotion to duty. He looked up as John entered his office.

"You wanted to see me, sir?"

"Yes." He didn't ask John to sit down. "I've been checking up on you, Weston. You're a clever man. The way you spot some of these smugglers is almost incredible. That egg trick, for example, and the one with the cigars, though that was obvious, shows that you have the right stuff in you. But..." He paused with well-timed deliberation.

"But what, sir?"

"Your bank account shows a steady decline of credit, Weston. For weeks now, you have been spending more than you earn." He leaned a little forward, the tips of his fingers placed carefully together. "What happens when your reserves are exhausted?"

"Isn't that my business, sir?"

"No, Weston, it isn't. And the sooner you get rid of that idea the better it will be for all of us." The sleek man relaxed back into his padded chair. "I don't have to paint a picture, Weston. You know the temptations a customs inspector has to face. I understand that with an extravagant wife to support life can be hard on the salary you receive. But let me warn you, Weston. If you should ever be tempted, and yield to that temptation, the penalties are severe. Do I make myself clear?"

"Too clear." John fought his rising temper. "Just because I choose to spend a little of my own money furnishing my apartment, you assume that I intend passing contraband. I find your suggestion insulting. If you don't trust me, then why don't you fire me and get it over?"

"You're a good man, Weston."

"Thanks. From your remarks, I had gathered otherwise. What do you do when you really mean to insult a man? Cut his throat?"

Strangely enough, the Superintendent didn't lose his temper. He smiled, leaning back in his padded chair and toying with a gold-tipped stylus. "You haven't answered my question, Weston. What happens when you have exhausted your financial reserves?"

"I'm not going to exhaust them." Suddenly his rising temper seemed to drain away, leaving him limp and trembling. "You don't have to lecture me, sir. I have already taken steps to ensure that my salary will be sufficient for my needs."

"Good." The sleek man smiled as he straightened in his chair. "Just so that we understand each other. Incidentally, you're due for a bonus. Not a large one, I'm afraid, but your discovery of that egg trick deserves some material recompense." He nodded towards the door. "That will be all, Weston. You may go now."

Outside the office, John felt almost sick with frustrated rage. Part of his mind tried to recognise the fact that the Super was only doing his duty, but the rest of him fumed with anger at the arrogance of the official who pried into private accounts and demanded explanations of how he spent his own money. At that moment, he could have cheerfully killed the man.

Madge was in when he arrived home, bathed and perfumed as he hadn't seen her for weeks, and she flung her arms around him as soon as he entered the door.

"Darling! Isn't it wonderful? Phil told me all about it."

"Did he?" John glanced to where the small man sat, his legs on the table, against a wall. "Did I win?"

"You did." Phil smiled as he straightened to his feet. "Good odds at that. Here." He threw a thick roll of credits onto the table. "Your hundred and three hundred more."

The sight of the money made John feel a lot better. He picked it up, riffling the credits, and smiled for the first time since his interview with the Superintendent. "Thanks, Phil. I won't forget this."

"But you're not going to stop now, are you darling?" Madge stared at the money with a hungry fascination. "This is our chance John! If you can win once, you can win again."

"Perhaps." John slipped the money into his pocket. "And then again, perhaps not. The time to stop is when you're winning."

"But you can't stop!" Madge stared at him, her eyes wide. "When Phil told me how much you'd won, I went out and bought a few things." She opened the cupboard door. "See?"

"Earth food!" John stared at the brightly labelled cans and the squat bottles. "Liquor! Cosmetics! Hell, Madge! Why did you do it?"

"Why not?" There was a hard defiance in her voice. "You didn't earn the money, did you? It was as good as a gift, the way you got it. Why shouldn't I have a few things to celebrate?" Abruptly she began to sob, the sound harsh and hideous in the sound-proofed room. "You don't love me anymore. You don't care how I feel. You and your money!" She made the word sound like a curse.

John sighed. "Well, that about takes care of the winnings." He shrugged and took the money from his pocket. "Here, Phil. See if you can do it again."

He did.

The four hundred climbed to seven—and Madge celebrated. The next time it dropped to three—and Madge went shopping to console herself. Then it climbed to nine, to twelve, then fell to eight—and each time, winning or losing, Madge went shopping, and each time John drew on his dwindling account to restock the gambling stake he had given to Phil. Finally the money had risen to a thousand, all he possessed, and his salary was booked to pay for dome and air rent. He ran all the way home to hear the news.

They didn't have to tell him. He could read it in his wife's face and he stared at Phil, a coldness growing in the pit of his stomach. "Lost?"

"Yes, John." The small man shrugged. "I warned you that I couldn't guarantee a win, but Madge said to put the lot on, so I did." He stared at his fingernails. "I'm sorry, John. But these things happen. We'll get it back next time."

"What next time?" John slumped tiredly into a chair. "I'm broke, Phil. Cleaned out. I haven't a credit left in reserve."

"Your bank account closed?"

"Almost." John felt sick as he remembered the Superintendent's suspicions. "It looks as though my job will be next."

"I could fix that for you," said Phil quickly. "How did you draw out the cash? In bulk?"

"Yes. A hundred or two at a time. Why?"

"You could have been buying things, couldn't you?"

"That's what I told the Super. I don't think that he believed me."

"He would if you sold them again."

"Sold what?" John gestured around the apartment. "Empty cans and liquor bottles? Waste perfume containers and discarded cosmetics? The whole lot wouldn't bring in a credit."

"Look, John." Phil leaned forward and spoke very quietly. "I know how you're fixed and, in a way, I feel that it's partly my fault." He raised a hand to silence John's protest. "You wouldn't have gambled if I hadn't given you the idea, but I didn't think that you were as flat as all that. Now listen. You've got a good job and you want to keep it, but if they check your accounts and find out just how much you've been spending lately..." He paused and looked at John. "Now do you get it?"

"Yes. With the gambling money I've spent more than I earn and more than I had in the bank. Unless..." He scribbled some figures on a scrap of paper. "Almost. If I hadn't won more than a thousand I'd be in the clear, but I did by a couple of hundred, and that puts me in it. If I tell them I won it gambling, I'll get fired anyway and I haven't the fare back to Earth. If I say nothing and they check, as they will do, then I've got to answer for it just the same. And if I don't tell I've been gambling, they'll think..."

'They will think that you've been passing contraband—and you know what that means." Phil shook his head. "I don't like to see you in this mess, John, and there's no need for you to stay in it. Not when there's a way out."

"How?"

"If you'd bought things with the money, and sold them at a profit, that would account for everything." Phil hesitated. "It will take a little money to fix, and more than I own to arrange the deal, but I know just the man who might do it."

"Who?"

"Does that matter, John?"

"Of course it doesn't." Madge flounced forward, her voice shrill and her lips twisted with impatience. "Do you think I want to be stranded here? Do you imagine that I want to be bonded to the yeast plant? Use your head, you fool. Phil is offering us both a way out of the mess you've gotten us into."

"So you suggest that this friend of yours fixes up some false bills and receipts, pays several hundred credits into my account, and smooths everything out for me." John looked at the small man. "Is that it?"

"That's right, John."

"Why?"

"Why?" Phil shrugged. "Does that matter? Maybe he thinks that it would be a good idea to have a friend in the right place. Maybe he just feels sorry for you. Or perhaps he thinks of it as a long-term investment. I assume that he will want some form of security, a cheque perhaps, one which he will never cash. An acknowledgment of gift or a deed of loan, something like that, just for security, of course."

"Of course," said John bleakly, and rubbed his throat. "I may be a fool, Phil. Sometimes I'm sure of it. But I'm not quite fool enough to put my head into a noose. The answer is no."

"It means ruin, John. Without your passage money to Earth, you'll both be bonded." The small man shrugged. "For you, it may even be worse."

"I see." John clenched his hands until the knuckles showed white beneath the skin. "You've been trying for this all along, haven't you?"

"Trying for what, John?" Phil smiled. "Look at it this way. A certain person has a friend, no matter who, and he would like this friend to pass the customs without any trouble. A simple thing when you look at it that way, and where's the harm? A few souvenirs, a curio or two, maybe something on which a heavy duty is payable. What it is doesn't matter. Now. Here you are in trouble, with the possibility of bonded labour for both you and your wife almost a certainty. You know how they operate, John? You'll see each other once a week, sleep in dormitories, eat filth and never know real comfort. More than that. You'll be able to see Earth and know that you'll never walk its green fields again. Prison wouldn't be as bad, John. At least you know when you'll be released, but bonded labour is for life. For life, John! Have you thought of that?"

"Stop it!"

"All you have to do is accept my friend's offer and restore your bank account. Then, when his friend arrives, you just pass him through. It's as simple as that. Just one small favour which won't cost you a deci-credit in return for financial security and freedom to go back home whenever you choose." The small man paused, and Madge wept as she clutched at John's knees, her bleached hair a tousled mess against his uniform. He stared down at her, trying to imagine her in the neutral grey of a bonded labourer, and shuddering as he visualised what must happen.

"It would be only for just the one time?"

"That's all, John. Just one favour in return for safety."

"You'll do it, John! Promise me that you'll do it?" Madge was hysterical as she grovelled on the carpet. "For God's sake, John, don't let me be bonded. I'll do anything you say, anything, but save me from that!"

Over her head, John stared at the small man's calm eyes.

"Tell your friend that I'll do it," he muttered. "For the one time only."

"Of course, John," said Phil, and rising, moved towards the door. He didn't smile until he was outside the room.

CHAPTER THREE

The man looked like some primitive monster as he walked slowly through the soft ooze clinging around his ankles. Plastic armour encased him from head to foot, a thin, tough, flexible covering with built-in gloves and boots, a sealed, self-service helmet, and oxygen supply. He waded through the soft mulch, moving carefully so as not to slip, and when he reached the shack, his face behind the transparent frontispiece was red and dripping with perspiration. Impatiently he waited as a man washed him down with a pressure hose, holding one hand well away from his body as if too-close contact with what he carried was the last thing he desired.

"Hell!" He swore with deep feeling and a trained invective as he removed the helmet. "I'm roasting in this thing."

"Did you get it?"

"Sure, I got it." He rested the sealed box on the loam as he wriggled out of the rest of the armour. "In the box, just as they gave it to me."

"They actually gave it to you?" The second man, a little wizened runt of a fellow, licked his lips as he prepared to ask the obvious question. Denton interrupted him.

"No. I didn't see them. The box was where I left it and I didn't stop to look around." He shuddered. "If ever there was a valley of hell, that spot is it. Even at that, I don't think I saw the worst. I kept getting the impression that there were things all around me, waiting, just watching for me to make a false move." He grunted as the little man held out a bottle of liquor. "Thanks." He tilted the container and gulped, his Adam's apple jerking in his throat as he swallowed the fiery spirit.

"Anyway, you got it." Jenner peered at the sealed box. "Is it safe?"

"I guess so. They wouldn't want to kill us. Not yet, anyway."
He joined the little man. "Contact Sam yet?"

"He radioed in about an hour ago. Said that he'd bring the
copter down at the edge of the Hotlands and take over the box."
Jenner looked at his big companion. "What's in it, Denton?"

"How the hell should I know?" The big man tilted the bottle
again. "All I know is that a man contacted us back at the trading
post and offered big money if we'd run this errand. If I'd have
known just what it was going to be like, I'd have asked double."
He frowned. "I might even have refused."

"Would you, Denton?"

"Yes." The big man shuddered again, as if at an unpleasant
memory. "I don't like Venus. There's too much mystery here, too
many nasty insects and unhealthy-looking plants. Why anyone
ever comes here at all beats me." He stared at the little man. "Why
did you come, Jenner?"

"No law here."

"Wanted?" The big man shrugged. "So am I, as far as I know.
Got drunk and jumped ship. Took all I could carry with me and
thought that I'd find a fortune in the Hotlands. Fortune!" He spat.
"What with swamp fever and bug bites, mud holes and fungi,
I'm lucky to be alive." He kicked the plastic armour into a heap
and stuffed it into a sack. "Come on. Let's get moving away from
here."

Together they broke camp, loading the heavy stuff on the
flatbed of a narrow trailer, and grunted as they hauled the primitive, balloon-tyred vehicle over the soft ground. Insects droned
around them, repelled by the thick salve both men had smeared
on their bodies, and the dull reports of exploding puffballs echoed
through the cathedral-like quietness of the moisture-laden Hotlands. It took them three days to reach a small clearing at the edge
of the treacherous swamps. Twice they had to unload the trailer,
dismantle it, and haul it piecemeal over fuming mud, skirting the
puckered orifices of silent geysers which at any moment could
spout mushroom-columns of boiling mud. Three times they aban-
doned everything but their weapons and the sealed box as a huge,

unseen shape lumbered with alien snortings through the tangled undergrowth. Once the little Jenner screamed with terror as a pale, lambent-white cup swung down from the trees and fastened over his head and shoulders. Denton blasted it with a searing tongue of flame before the carnivorous plant could emit its acid juices, but the episode left the little man so shaken that they had to rest for almost half a day.

Finally they emerged into the clearing and made camp, the big man breaking out supplies while Jenner connected up the transceiver.

"Can you contact him?"

"Trying." Sweat oozed from the little man's forehead as he tapped the key and listened for a reply. "These damned batteries are half dead." He grunted. "Got him!"

"Ask him how long."

"Tomorrow." Jenner stared at the big man. "Anything else?"

"Tell him to bring a case of whisky, he can take it out of our cash." The big man licked his lips. "Space! When I get back to Aphrodite, I'll throw a binge which will make history. Tell him that, Jenner, and tell him not to be late."

The little man worked the key with skilled fingers, listened for a moment, tapped again, then slipped off the headphones. "I wish we had a proper radio. This gadget might be small, but it's hell having to work a key." He began replacing the transceiver in its case. "Sam says to light a red smoke flare at midday."

"Is he bringing the whisky?"

"He said so." Jenner snapped the catch on the damp-proof case. "I wonder what's in the box, Denton. Did you see anything which might give you a clue?"

"No." The big man slapped at a buzzing insect. "I set it down on the rock as directed when I got back, after maybe an hour, the lid was closed." He shuddered. "That was the longest hour I've ever lived. I didn't stop to argue or try to be smart. All I wanted to do was to get out of the valley and back to camp. I wouldn't go in there again for double what we were promised."

"Thirty thousand credits," murmured Jenner, and there was something feral in the way he licked his lips. "A man could get back to Earth with that much money." He glanced towards the tent in which the sealed box rested. "Whatever is in that box must be worth more than we guess. Suppose we asked for more?" He stared at the big man. "We could get another ten thousand if we held out."

"Perhaps."

"Well?"

"I'm satisfied with my cut. Fifteen thousand will buy all the rotgut I can drink and I don't want trouble. What's the good of money to a dead man?"

"What's the good of life without money?" Jenner yawned. "Space, I feel tired. I think I'll hit the sack and dream of what I'm going to do with that thirty thousand."

"Fifteen thousand," said Denton tightly. "We share, remember?"

"That's right." Jenner yawned again. "You take first watch?"

"Sure."

"Right. Call me when you get tired." The little man nodded and vanished within the tent, moving the assembled gear around to make a bed. After a while, his movements ceased and the sounds of his heavy breathing mingled with the slow, continuous drip of rain from the surrounding trees.

Denton hunched down beside the trailer, resting his broad shoulders against one of the balloon tyres, and listened to the droning silence of the Hotlands. Once, he started as a puffball exploded with a dull report, then relaxed as he realised it was too far off for the cloud of emitted spores to threaten him. As he sat, he thought of Jenner.

He didn't trust the little man. He had met him in a dive at Aphrodite and the two had joined up, pooling their equipment and trying to make a living by collecting rare medicinal plant-pods in the treacherous swamps. At irregular intervals they returned to the city to barter their harvest for supplies and liquor, equipment and compressed food. It was during one of these trips that they had met the stranger with his glittering proposition. At the time it had seemed simple. Merely venture into the unknown regions of the valley, set down an open box, return after an hour and collect it again. For thirty thousand credits it had seemed a simple task, but now Denton wasn't so sure.

He had done most of the work, and his skin crawled as he remembered the silent menace of the valley. He had sweated in his plastic armour, risking his neck every step of the way, and all Jenner had done was to wait and operate the radio. It wasn't fair that he should share equally. It wasn't fair that he should share at all. He shifted uncomfortably against the swollen tyre as he thought about it. If he didn't have to share the cash, if Jenner had died that time the carnivorous plant had got him...

Thirty thousand credits was twice as much as fifteen—and the opportunity might never occur again to earn so much with so little effort. He didn't trust the little man. There was something in the way he smiled, a furtive expression in his red-rimmed eyes. If Jenner could be—eliminated? Slowly Denton slipped the blaster from the holster at his belt and checked the load.

From the tent came a snorting grunt, the sound of a body turning over, and a long, whistling sigh. Denton froze, the weapon in his hand levelled at the small tent, then, slowly, he replaced it in his holster. A blaster would do too much damage, would sear and ruin the structure together with its contents—and the sealed box was within the tent. A knife hung at his belt, a wickedly shaped length of razor-edged steel, and he drew it, testing the needle point on the ball of his thumb.

Softly he moved towards the tent and the snoring man.

Inside it was dim, almost dark after the brightness outside, but he could make out a huddled figure lying to one side. He tensed, listening to the grunting breath of a man far gone in sleep, then, the knife a glittering arc as it flashed downwards, Denton flung himself forward. Twice he stabbed, driving the keen blade with all the power of his great back and shoulders, slamming the long blade up to the hilt in something soft and yielding. A third time he lifted the steel, then paused, swearing in amazed disbelief as he stared at the bundle of armour and baled supplies lying where he thought a man had lain helpless in sleep.

"Surprised, Denton?"

"What?" The big man spun, his eyes widening as he tried to peer through the gloom. "Jenner?"

"Who else?" There was a snarl in the little man's voice. "I'm over here, Denton—if you're interested." He squatted, a crouched figure, at one side of the tent, the sealed box beside him and a slender-barrelled high-velocity pistol in his hand.

"You!" The big man swore, his hand drawing back as if to throw the knife, then dropped it as he stared into the tiny orifice of the H.V. pistol barrel. "I..." He licked suddenly dry lips. "I thought..."

"You thought that thirty thousand was better than fifteen." Jenner chuckled. "A funny thing, Denton, I thought the same." He raised the pistol. "Goodbye, Denton."

"No!" Sweat oozed from the big man's forehead. "You can't kill me, Jenner! Not like this! You can have my share, I promise you, but don't kill me." He lunged forward, both hands outstretched in mute pleading. "Please, Jenner, I..." He stiffened, a shocked expression twisting his features, and on his chest tiny red flowers bloomed in lethal splendour. Even as the thin, spiteful cracks of the pistol faded into silence, the big man died, the life blasted out of him by the hydrostatic shock of the tiny, incredibly fast slugs from Jenner's pistol.

Calmly the little man slipped his weapon into its hidden holster and settled down to sleep.

The jetcopter arrived the next day, guided by the tall, wavering column of red smoke from the flare bomb. Jenner watched it drift down to a landing, not moving until the cabin door had swung aside and a man leapt into the clearing.

"Jenner! Denton! Where are you?"

"Sam?"

"That's me." The pilot frowned as he stared at the silent "Where are you?"

"Here." Jenner stepped from the edge of the clearing, his hand resting carelessly on the weapon at his belt. "You got the stuff?"

"Sure. Where's Denton?"

"He's around." Jenner held out his hand. "Where's the money?"

"Not so fast." Sam narrowed his eyes as he stared at the little man. "Where's the box?"

"I've got it."

"Then pass it over. The quicker I get away from here, the better. Now give!"

Jenner didn't move. He stood, his hand resting on the butt of his blaster, his little eyes flickering over the pilot and the sleek machine behind him. Overhead, the wide rotors revolved like a giant fan, the faint breeze caused by their passage through the moisture-laden air cooling the sweat on his brow. He grinned.

"You know," he said casually. "That box must be pretty valuable. I'm beginning to think that Denton and me are getting the short end of the deal. Anything that valuable must be worth a lot more than a lousy thirty thousand credits."

"I wouldn't know about that." Sam held out his hand. "You're wasting time. Give me the box."

"I reckon that we should get at least fifty thousand." Jenner grinned at the pilot. "In fact, I'm certain of it."

"What's that got to do with me? I haven't got fifty thousand."

"You could get it, Sam." Jenner glanced at the jetcopter. "You could go and get it now."

"You think so?" Sam shrugged and turned towards the machine. "Forget it. The people I work for won't pay that much. If you're not satisfied with the original deal, we'll call the whole thing off." He glanced over the clearing. "Where's Denton? What does he think about this?"

"Don't worry about Denton." Jenner licked his lips as the pilot stepped towards the machine. "You going to get the money?"

"No."

"What's it to you, Sam? All you need to do is to take a message and, when I collect, I'll cut you in ten thousand. It's easy money, Sam. Easy for the two of us." He stepped forward. "Well?"

"I don't know." The pilot frowned as he looked at Jenner. "The two of us, you say? What about Denton?"

"He's been taken care of." Jenner jerked his head towards the tent. "Forget him. What do you say?"

"Get the box. I'll take you back with me and you can do your own bargaining. If you can persuade them to pay you an extra twenty thousand, I get ten. Is that it?"

"Yes." Jenner grinned and moved towards the edge of the clearing. When he returned, he held the sealed box in one hand and his drawn blaster in the other.

Sam stared at the weapon. "What's the matter? Don't you trust me?"

"I don't trust anyone. That's why I'm still alive." Jenner halted a few yards from the machine. "Before we go any further, Sam, where is the thirty thousand?"

"I've got it. Get aboard if you're going to and let's get moving."

"Not so fast." The blaster tilted in the little man's hand. "The money, Sam."

"You'll get it."

"I want it now."

"So that you can burn me down and take over the 'copter?" The pilot shook his head. "Put away that blaster, Jenner. I don't reckon on getting burned down once you've got the money. I'm not that stupid."

"No?" Jenner laughed. "Take the box." He put it down and walked a few yards away. "Now get me the money. We'll make a level swap, Sam, and don't try anything clever. I can shoot the rotors off that 'copter before you could get twenty feet in the air. And when you bring out the cash, don't bring a weapon." He gestured with his gun. "Hurry, now."

"Just in case you're thinking of burning me down, Jenner," said the pilot quietly. "I'm the only man on Venus who knows who would be interested in buying that box. Just remember that." He turned and walked towards the machine and, when he returned, held a wrapped package in his hand. "Here." He threw it towards Jenner. "Count it. While you're doing that, I'll take the box."

Jenner nodded. Tucking the blaster under one arm he fumbled with the package, tearing at the seal and snarling with impatience. "Why the hell did they have to wrap it up like this?" He glared at Sam, now almost at the open cabin door. "Don't shut that thing. If you do, I'll blast it open."

"I won't." Sam stood at the open door, leaning half out of the cabin. "What's holding you up?"

"This damn seal! I..." With abrupt suddenness, the package seemed to dissolve in his hands. A cloud plumed from it, a thick yellow cloud gushing from the ripped seal and spraying all over the head and shoulders of the little man.

He screamed.

He shrieked with the agony of burning eyes and seared flesh, of bursting ears and dissolving membranes. He groaned, staggering about the clearing while, all over him, like a great fluffy ball of delicate yellow cotton, the swirling cloud grew and thickened around his flesh.

Hastily, Sam shut the cabin door, gunning his engine so that the whirling blades of the rotor sent a blast of air all over the machine. With a sick fascination, he stared through the plastic windows at the thing still lurching aimlessly about the clearing. The cloud had gone by now, the swirling mass of spores burying themselves deep into living flesh, taking root and growing with incredible swiftness. Even as he watched, Jenner stumbled, fell, twitched once, then sagged in the merciful oblivion of death.

Over him, a thick, yellow, almost lace-like fungus heaved slightly as it dissolved the flesh and bone beneath. Little pods formed, burst, the released spores, which drifted until beaten down by the mist-like rain. Not until the heaving mass of growth had died, reduced to a thin yellow film on the black loam, did the pilot finally turn from the window.

He didn't look at the box as he lifted the machine.

CHAPTER FOUR

Aphrodite rested on the levelled peak of a mountain, a peculiar collection of the ultra-modern and the primitive, with the wide expanse of the spaceport in startling contrast to the crude, leaf-thatched hutments clustered on the lower slopes. Sam brought the jetcopter down in a wide circle, skilfully riding the uprising thermal currents and avoiding the space lanes. He poised over the central square, slid around the towering spire of the Universal Trading Corporation, and drifted gently down into the courtyard of a rambling, glass-brick and stressed-concrete structure. Switching off the engines, he picked up the sealed box and jumped from the machine. A man met him just as he was about to enter the building.

"Any luck?"

"No. I couldn't get a glimpse of one." Sam jerked his thumb at a closed door. "Merrill in?"

"Yes. Waiting for you, I think. Shall I take care of the 'copter?"

"Might as well. I won't be going out again today, anyway." Sam yawned. "Maybe I'll have better luck tomorrow." He grinned after the man, then, squaring his shoulders, pushed open the door and entered a small, sound-proofed room.

Merrill stared at him from behind his wide desk. A strange man, this Merrill. An old, almost withered man, with twisted limbs and thin, claw-like hands. Smouldering eyes peered from sunken sockets and the glow-lights illuminating the windowless room reflected in shimmers of white and yellow from his naked scalp. He rested in a great chair, almost lost against the soft padding, and about him there was an aura as of things long dead. He stared at Sam as the pilot closed the door.

"Well?" The voice was a dry whisper, as if the throat had long since dried and left only scraped bone and stringy tissue.

"I got it." Sam set the sealed box down on the desk.

"The men?"

"Dead. The spore-trap got one, the little one. Jenner, his name was. He'd killed his companion before I got there."

"Are you certain of that?"

"Yes."

"Did you see the body?"

"No, but I didn't have to. I..."

"Fool!" Anger, the more terrible because of the rustling voice, stemmed from the withered figure. "How often must you be told? It is imperative that both of the men should die. You have been careless."

"I was careful," corrected the pilot. "Denton was dead before I got there. They had obviously quarrelled before I came, probably over the division of spoils. I had no chance to see his body, and after the spore-trap had been sprung, I didn't want to." He touched the box. "Anyway, what are you worried about? Here it is, sealed, delivered and free. What more do you want?"

"I want efficiency!" Merrill glared at the pilot. "I gave you orders to make certain that both of those men were eliminated. I expect my orders to be obeyed!"

Sam shrugged and fumbled in the pocket of his leather jacket. From a crumpled package, he took a cigarette, puffed it to glowing life, and blew a thin streamer of blue smoke across the desk. "You want to get a new boy?"

"What do you mean?"

"I'm a hunter. I've been other things in my time, but an office boy wasn't one of them. Guard your tongue, Merrill, or you can do your own dirty work." Sam dragged at his cigarette. "Those men are dead, all right. No need to worry about that. I dropped a heat bomb on their camp before I left and no one can traverse the Hotlands without equipment and supplies." He sat on the edge of the desk. "What about tomorrow?"

"What about it?"

"There's a party coming in, isn't there? They've booked up a hunting party and I'm supposed to have located the game for them. I haven't. I couldn't look for quarry and pick up the box at the same time, and I had to be careful. What happens now?"

"Carter located a Tryplizard yesterday. He marked it and you'll be able to locate it with a tracer. Use that."

"What about Carter? It's his quarry."

"I've seen to that. Carter's got a couple of days leave, never mind how I fixed it, but he won't worry if you track his Tryp." Merrill smiled, a thin twitching of paper-lips. "Foresight, my friend. Foresight."

"Fair enough." Sam let blue smoke trickle through his nostrils. He touched the sealed box. "What happens now?"

"We get it to Earth."

"Earth?" Sam shook his head. "Why?"

"That's none of your business. Just do as you are told and forget what you've done as soon as you do it." Merrill touched the container with reverent hands. "I don't know all about it, Sam, but there's money in it, big money. That's all you need worry about."

"I agree." Sam crushed out the butt of his cigarette. "When do I get paid?"

"Later."

"That's not good enough, Merrill. I've done the job and I want the cash. And don't try paying me off with a spore-trap like you did Jenner. I won't like that."

"You'll get paid."

"Sure I will." Sam rose and picked up the sealed box. "I'll just hang on to this until I do."

"You fool!" Merrill half-rose from his chair, looking like a distorted monkey as he clutched the box. "You can't take that. You'll ruin everything. Give it back to me."

"When I get paid."

"I see." Merrill slumped back into his chair, his thin mouth bitter. "You're just like all the rest. Money. That's all you think about. That's the beginning and ending of your life." He paused and his smouldering eyes seemed to stare past the pilot, through the sound-proofed walls, and out to somewhere in the steaming Hotlands. "Isn't there anyone anywhere who can think past his own personal pockets? Isn't there anyone who will do something for the sake of an ideal?" He stared at the pilot. "I can't pay you yet, Sam. I haven't got the money."

"What!" Anger twisted the hard features of the hunter. "You promised..."

"I know what I promised, and you will be paid, but I can't pay you now." The old man leaned over the wide desk. "Listen, you fool! Once this box reaches Earth, we will be worth millions. But payment is strictly C.O.D. Now do you understand?"

"So I've been taken for a sucker!" Sam glanced at the old man. "Is that why you paid off those two swamp-rats with a spore-trap?"

"They were scum, of no account but to venture into the valley and collect the box. They had to die, Sam, you know that, if for no other reason than to keep them from talking." Merrill stared down at his hands. "I'm not used to begging, Sam, but this time I'm asking you a favour. I've sunk all I own into this venture, every credit the syndicate has and, unless I can collect on the goods, I'm ruined. Play along with me and you'll get double what I promised, I swear it!'

"So you've dipped into the syndicate's funds, too, have you?" Sam grinned. "If they ever find out, they'll tie a beacon to you, turn you loose in the Hotlands, and hunt you down with H. V. rifles." He wiped at his eyes as he stared at the box. "If you took a risk like that," he whispered, "then this box must be a financial gold mine. What's in it, Merrill? What's in it?"

"I don't know."

"What?"

"It's the truth, Sam. I just don't know." The old man sighed and something of the burning fire in his eyes seemed to flash momentarily and then fade to bleak and lifeless ash. "I was propositioned, never mind by whom, and I saw the chance to make a killing. You know what we do here. We run hunting trips for tourists who want to kill some really big game. We are the one organisation able to go into the Hotlands with no questions asked. The proposition was simple. Merely pick up a box from the valley and deliver it to Earth. I've covered all the tracks, those two men who did the actual pickup can't be connected with us here, and there are no long absences to account for, either for jetcopters or personnel. We're safe, Sam, safe. And all we have to do now is to deliver the goods."

"And run smack into the customs inspection at Luna Station." Sam snorted with disgust. "I'm surprised at you, Merrill. Didn't you think of that?"

"I did."

"Then what are you going to do?" Sam lit a fresh cigarette. "You can't fire it to Earth in a small rocket. For one thing, it would get lost, and even if you fixed a radio beacon to it, the guards would locate and find it. You can't land on Earth unless you pass through the station. If you try it, you'll have a guard ship on your tail as soon as you break the radar screens. You can't just explode in on a free orbit. The atmospheric friction will burn it to ash. And, anyway, I assume that you want to find it again." He stared at the glowing tip of his cigarette. "That leaves Luna Station, and you wouldn't have a hope in hell of smuggling it in past customs."

"No?"

"No." Sam stared at the old man. "Not unless..." He snapped his fingers. "You've fixed an inspector! Is that it?"

"Perhaps."

"So that's it!" Sam whistled. "Boy, if I only knew which one, I'd make a fortune in one trip." He shook his head. "Still no good. They have a second check on Earth arrival."

"Admitted, but how good is it?" Merrill smiled. "Assume that there is a small landing field, in China perhaps, or in one of the more primitive countries. Assume an official who is perhaps... tired, shall we say? Careless? Anyway, he knows that the Luna Station checks with remarkable thoroughness and it would be only human nature for him to assume that they did their job properly." Merrill shrugged. "The Earth check is simple once Luna Station is taken care of."

"It might work at that." Sam squinted through the smoke pluming from his cigarette. "What is in the box, Merrill?"

"I told you, I don't know."

"Playing it smart?" Sam shrugged. "I can make a guess."

"Any man can guess." Merrill stared at the pilot through hooded eyes. "Sometimes it isn't wise to guess at all."

"Threatening me, Merrill?"

"No, Sam, not threatening. Just warning."

"You don't scare me." The pilot dragged at his cigarette. "A small box, sealed, straight from the valley. A box worth millions on Earth. I'd guess spores of some kind. I'd go even further." He grinned at the old man. "Narcotics?"

"I don't know."

"For a man who doesn't know what he's handling, you're taking a hell of a lot on trust." The pilot stuck the cigarette between his lips and picked up the box. "There's one sure way of finding out." He grunted as his fingers strained at the box.

Merrill smiled as he watched. "You won't open it, Sam."

"No? Wait until I get some tools on the job. I'll get it open."

"Perhaps." Merrill twisted his thick lips in a grin. "Remember what happened to Jenner?"

"The spore-trap? Sure, I remember. I..." He gulped and gently set down the box. "You mean..."

"I don't mean anything, Sam, but that box came from the valley, and who knows what may be down there." Merrill stared at the smooth metal. "Personally, I don't want to find out. All I want is my money."

"And so do I."

"Naturally, and you'll get it...as soon as this box is delivered on Earth."

"Yes." Sam brooded as he smoked, his eyes hard and thoughtful. "Who's going to deliver it, Merrill?"

"A contact."

"Obviously. But who?" The pilot stared at the old man. "How can we trust him? How do I know when I'm due to collect? What if he runs out on us?"

"He won't."

"I'm not so sure about that." The pilot looked worried. "Earth is a big place. He could take the cash and hide himself and we'd never have a chance of finding him." He dragged on the cigarette. "I don't like it, Merrill. I don't like it at all."

"Neither do I," admitted the old man. "But what can we do? I'm too old to go, and besides, I'm needed here. Someone must deliver it, and we've got to trust the man who does." He shrugged. "There's no other way."

"Yes there is." Sam crushed out his cigarette and stared at the old man. "I can deliver and collect."

"You?" Merrill shook his head. "I'm sorry, Sam, but that's impossible."

"Why?"

"Your work is here. You've no good reason to return to Earth and you've no experience with customs. Those inspectors are shrewd. They can tell if a man is smuggling by the way he looks at his fingers, the way he breathes, a dozen little ways. You wouldn't stand a chance."

"You said the inspector was fixed. I can walk through the same as anyone else."

"Admitted, but..."

"There are no buts, Merrill. I take the box or it doesn't go at all." Sam rose to his feet, one hand on the container. "Well?"

"You really want to go, Sam?"

"Yes."

"Very well, then." Merrill sighed. "I'll arrange transportation and you can pass the rumour that you're going back to visit your mother or something like that." He hesitated. "One other thing, Sam. I trust you as much as I have to, but no more than that. Don't try and get smart ideas. I've friends on Earth, and they will take care of you if you try to cross me. Understood?"

"Warning me, Merrill?"

"No, Sam. This time I'm just telling you what will happen unless you play it straight. Don't take me for too big a fool. And, remember, the money will be paid into the Interplanetary Bank when you deliver, not in cash."

"Will it?" Sam didn't trouble to hide his contempt. "I know better than that, Merrill. This is a hush-hush deal and you know it. You wouldn't be fool enough to leave a trail from the buyers of this stuff straight to you, and neither would they." He chuckled as he headed for the door. "Don't worry about it, Merrill. You can trust me. You've got no choice."

He was still chuckling as the door closed behind him.

CHAPTER FIVE

Merrill sighed and rose slowly from his chair. He moved with a painful awkwardness, dragging a twisted leg and lurching rather than walking towards the blank surface of a wall. A panel slid aside as he rested his palm against a sensitised plate, the electronic mechanism recognising his palm print, and he passed through into a small instrument-cluttered room. A man looked up from where he sat before a microscope. A tall, thin man with receding hair and weak eyes staring from behind thick lenses. He smiled as he saw the box.

"Everything all right, Merrill?"

"So far." The old man set down the container and slumped in a chair. "Are we doing the right thing, Fenshaw? Are we?"

The tall man swung around on his swivel seat, snapping off the brilliant microscope light and blinking his eyes to relieve them of strain. He stared thoughtfully at the old man, then, rising, ran long fingers over the smooth metal of the box. Around him, in pots and sealed containers, a wild profusion of plant life rested on ranked shelves. He stared at the growths, his weak eyes glowing with the peculiar gleam of the utter fanatic, and it was not until Merrill repeated his question that he answered.

"The right thing? Who can tell? Did Madame Curie do the 'right thing'? Did Pasteur? Did Lister? Those at the front line of science must always be accused of that. It is one of the crosses they must bear, those who seek to widen the fields of human knowledge and ease the burden of human care." He sighed as he stared down at the sealed box. "Was Sam difficult?"

"No." Merrill twitched his lips in a smile. "Like most of the men on Venus, he knows little of psychology. It was surprisingly simple to get him to volunteer."

"He hopes to trick us, of course?"

"Of course." Merrill smiled again. "I should be disappointed in him if he did not. I like to deal with a man who has simple motivations. It is always so simple. It is almost possible to see the wheels spin in their empty, foolish heads." He sighed. "Why are men such fools, Fenshaw?"

"That question ranks with the one about truth," said the tall man quietly. "What is truth? Answer that and you answer all. Are men foolish because they spend their lives in an unceasing quest for wealth, or does the quest make them foolish? I do not know. I do not care to know. Science has no such paradoxes and I am a scientist." He said it with a peculiar arrogance, as another man might say "I am a king" but there was a simple sincerity about him which robbed the words of their arrogance. He touched the box again. "Does Sam know the truth?"

"No. He thinks that the swampers merely collected the box."

"Good." Fenshaw stood for a moment, deep in thought, his eyes misty behind their thick lenses. "This is a dangerous thing we do, Merrill. Are you sure that you have no regrets?"

"I have no regrets." The old man hunched forward in his chair. "That is, I have none if the promises are to be kept. And they will be kept, won't they, Fenshaw?"

"Yes."

"How do you know?"

"How do you know that beyond the clouds lie the stars? The thin man shrugged. "I have faith. So far, everything they have told me has turned out to be just as predicted. The advances I have made—the spore-trap is but one—and the questions I have solved! Merrill, you can't even begin to guess. Venus is a tremendous biological laboratory, a vast conglomeration of experiments designed to produce the optimum life form. We have only seen the byproducts, the offshoots and discards. Soon we shall see the real."

"Perhaps." Merrill shivered as if the touch of a cold wind. "I take your word for it, Fenshaw, as I have done since you came to me with your wild ideas, but even the whole idea seems incredible."

"Why should it, Merrill? Just because intelligent life on Earth has resulted in an animal, does it mean that intelligence must be confined to a beast? It has long been known that plants have, if not intelligence, at least awareness of light and dark, of heat and near objects and far. The common bean can sense the pole up which it will climb and move towards it. Any seed knows in which direction to send out the root, and which to send out the shoot. Have you ever seen a flower follow the sun? And what of the carnivorous plants? They have long been known on Earth, and there are others, many others. No, Merrill, there is nothing incredible about what we have discovered."

"Perhaps not." The old man shook his head. "But why are they so insistent on sending the contents of that box to Earth? Why at all?"

"They use us because of all creatures we are intelligent and mobile. We are the only ones they can use, and we, you and I, can be glad of it. As to why they want that box sent to Earth, I've told you a dozen times. Communication. An extension of the group mind." He sighed as he stared at the old man. "You know the bargain, Merrill. We dare not fail in our part. If we do, they will know and..."

"Yes." The old man wiped his forehead with a trembling and stared at his moist palm. "Do you think they can do it, Fenshaw? Can they take this ruined body and restore it to youth? Can they?"

"I have faith that they can." Fenshaw turned and stared at one of the plants. "It is only a matter of adjustment, a delicate alteration of the cellular tissue, a breaking down and elimination of waste deposits. Plants do it all the time, an old tree is a fit tree, and will remain so until attacked by disease. But the analogy is poor and has no relation to the incredible efficiency of those who live in the valley."

"Have you ever seen one?" Merrill looked curiously at the man. "You seem to know more about them than any other living man. How did you obtain that knowledge?"

"Does it matter?" Fenshaw smiled. "I offer you a new life, Merrill. The chance to be young again, to feel the hot blood running through your veins and the surge and pulse of health straightening your limbs. That is your reward for doing what you have agreed to do. Mine?" He shrugged. 'The same, perhaps, or perhaps a little more. I do not know as yet which I shall choose, but one thing we are sure of. They are generous, Merrill. They can afford to be, for without us they are helpless to extend their lines of communication to a new world. Only men can cross space."

"Yes," said Merrill, and bit his withered lips. "I wish there were some other way. We are so few and there is not enough money, nowhere near enough. Two men have died already, and there are others to be paid." He looked at the thin man. "You have the narcotics?"

"Yes." Fenshaw opened a drawer and lifted out a plastic cylinder. "Here. Tszenga dust. One pinch on any of the absorbent membranous surfaces and a man is in his own private heaven." He scowled down at the opaque container. "Filth!"

"But valuable." Merrill took the cylinder and rolled it between his palms. "What do we care about the addicts? This will pay for the box to get past inspection. What the contact does with it is no concern of ours." He sighed as he slipped the cylinder in his pocket. "I wish that we didn't have to do this. Why can't we notify the authorities? They could send out a scientific team and examine the..." he hesitated. "What do you call them, Fenshaw?"

"Call them?" The thin man shrugged. "Normally I think of them as the most advanced form of life possible. But a name?" He shrugged. "If you insist on a name, why not call them the Delphi?"

"The Delphi?" Merrill frowned. "Why? I catch the reference to the oracle, but wouldn't it be more correct to call them by the singular?"

"I am. Would you call them the Delphis?" Fenshaw seemed irritated. "You must never forget that there are no individuals. All are part of the whole, linked by actual physical contact as well as a group consciousness. In essence, they are like fungi, apparently individual growths, but each joined together by the sub-surface spawn beds." Fire sparkled in his weak eyes. "They are wonderful, Merrill. They are true scientists, with the correct detachment and the willingness to experiment. They have waited in the valley for uncounted years, distributing their spores over every part of Venus so that they practically cover the entire planet." He stared at the old man. "You don't believe that, do you, Merrill?"

"If what you say is true," said the old man slowly, "why haven't we found traces of them? If they cover the planet, then why haven't we discovered them before? Any organism such as you describe must surely have been found by now."

"It has."

"But..."

"Remember I said that they cover the entire planet, but I didn't say that the intelligences themselves were obvious. They are not. But you have seen the puffballs, Merrill. You have heard of the carnivorous plants, the sting trees, the whip vines. You know how hard it is for any expedition to venture far into the Hotlands." The thin man smiled. "There is your answer, Merrill."

"Incredible!" The old man stared in amazement. "You to say that all those trees, the fungi, everything we see about us is a part of the Delphi?" He shook his head. "I can't believe it."

"If you were an ant," said Fenshaw coldly, "and you had climbed first on a man's hand, and then on his face, would you believe that both parts belonged to the one organism? If you were a germ travelling from the heart to the brain, would the same thing strike you? It is all a matter of size, Merrill. Size and conception. There is no limit to plant growth, no limit to its size or its extent. On Venus, the Delphi learned to destroy opposition and, with an entire planet to spread in..." He spread his hands. "What's so incredible about it?"

"But the insects, the animals. Didn't they destroy plant life?"

"To a certain extent, perhaps, comparable to the bite of a flea to a normal man, but they do something else. They spread the spores, pollinate the plants, convert the fruits, and, perhaps most important all, act as mobile appendages to the immobile intelligence." The thin man leaned forward. "Exactly as we are doing, Merrill. In just the same way."

"Then why don't we notify the scientists of what you have found?" The old man half-rose from his chair then slowly relaxed again as the scientist glowered down at him. "I know what you're thinking, Fenshaw, but this thing is too big to keep as a private thing. Think of it, man! Just think of it!"

"I am thinking of it." The thin man made no attempt to hide his bitterness. "You know what would happen if we did as you suggest? The scientists would come, of course. They would come in their dozens and with them would come the tools and instruments of their trade. They would dig, cut, test. They would call in the military and burn a path into the valley. They would dissect the Delphi, cut then apart in cold, so-called scientific detachment, and they just wouldn't be able to accept the fact that anything not of flesh and blood could be intelligent. They would come and they would be beaten back by an organism trying to defend itself. Then they would scream for help and, because Man must be dominant wherever he is, war would be declared on Venus. They wouldn't call it war, of course. To them, it would be an interesting problem of how to clear the Hotlands, and they would use everything they possess to do it. Acid, fire, atomic dusts, chemicals, supersonic vibration, the works. And when they had finished, the greatest repository of knowledge ever known would lie in broken ruin, oozing sap, torn tendrils and ruptured sacs. The Delphi would be dead."

He paused and sweat shone on his high forehead and he gasped for breath as a man would gasp who has run for many miles. "I have thought of this before, Merrill. I have thought of it and what would happen if I announced my discovery, and I think that our way is the best and only way."

Merrill frowned. What Fenshaw had told him wasn't wholly a surprise. He had lived too long on Venus to be surprised at anything the veiled planet could produce, and the theory of a planet-wide plant intelligence was one way to account for the utter lack of any native—humanoid native, that is—life. He sat brooding as the thin man worked among his plants, taking cellular samples, slicing them, mounting them on slides and preparing them for microscopic inspection. Fenshaw was always working. Driving himself in a seemingly desperate race against time, searching among the alien life forms for—what? Merrill didn't know and, when he came to think of there was little about the scientist that he did know.

He had met him five years before. A fever-ravaged ruin on the edge of the Hotlands, without equipment or supplies. Where he came from was a mystery, and he never volunteered an explanation. He had said that his name was Fenshaw, that he was a biologist interested in plant life and alien life forms. Merrill had given him a job, then, as the man had showed himself useful in a dozen ways, had set him up in the laboratory. The syndicate for which he worked, an interplanetary group of financiers who had set up a big-game hunting organisation for sportsmen with too much money and an urge to kill something really big, had admitted Fenshaw's usefulness when he had designed the quarry tracer system. A spotter would hover over the Hotlands in a jetcopter, find a huge beast, fire a radioactive-containing shell at the thing's hide, and then it could be traced down by the beam-counters for anytime up to a month afterwards. The synthetic radioactive was harmless to the beast and it cut down the hunt-time when parties arrived for their sport.

It was after that when Fenshaw had fed Merrill's secret dream.

The lure had been simple and, to a man who was old, with a body twisted by accident and disease, irresistible. Health! Youth! The chance to start over and live again. And the price? Merely delivery of a box to a rendezvous on Earth. The breaking of a technical law. The smuggling of something which could be contraband, and then again, need not. Seeds, perhaps, or spores, a little something from Venus to Earth. Once the dream had taken hold and the anticipated pleasures of a restored youth tasted, even though only in imagination. Merrill was lost.

Death—other men's death—came easily after that.

He stirred and looked at the thin man. "You're sure that they will know when the box reaches Earth?"

"They will know."

"How? It's a long way and, from what you say, the Delphi don't use radio. How will they know that we have done our part of the bargain?"

"Telepathy." Fenshaw paused in his preparation of a slide. "Surprised? You needn't be. Thought is basically the same as radio. Much finer, of course, and it is essential that the 'transmitter' and 'receiver' be in perfect tune, but it is possible. In fact, it has been demonstrated that even humans are able to transmit and pick up thoughts. The Delphi will know by telepathy."

"I don't get it." Merrill felt the gnawings of doubt. "How can seeds, or spores, and that is what I assume is in the box, be able to send messages across the void like that? For one thing, even if a full-grown Delphi could do it, the seeds aren't full grown. I don't like it, Fenshaw. I don't like it at all."

"You want to back out?" The thin man shrugged. "You can if you want to. There's nothing to stop you now. Just get rid of the box, pay off Sam and ignore the contact on Luna. Simple."

"Yes," said Merrill bitterly. "Simple. Just forget the two dead men. Pay Sam with money I haven't got and just tell the Luna contact, the man who expects narcotic as his pay for arranging the fixed inspector, that it was all a mistake. Damn you, Fenshaw! You know I can't back out now."

"Then why talk about it?" said the thin man coldly. He smiled, a writhing of his lips as he tried to get friendly warmth into his usually bitter tones. "What's the matter with you, man? You can't back out now that we are so near to success. The hard work's all but been done and once Sam delivers the box to that place on Earth, we'll collect our reward. Think of it, Merrill. You'll be young again. That twisted leg of yours will be straight and strong as it used to be. You'll have a second chance at life, and you'll have all your knowledge and experience to give you a start. I can't understand why you hesitate."

"It sounds good," said Merrill slowly and felt his heart leap at thought of what the other man offered. "It almost seems too good." He bit his lips. "If I could only be sure."

"You must trust the Delphi. And what have you to lose? On the one hand, you have everything it is possible for anyone to offer. On the other, you will merely stay as you are. It's not even a gamble, Merrill. It's a gift."

"Beware the Greeks," muttered the old man. He looked at the box. "What about Sam?"

"I'll take care of Sam," promised the thin man grimly. "We'll have no blackmailers on our tail, and Sam is a born extortionist." He smiled down at the old man. "Feel better now?"

"Yes, but if I could only be sure."

"You can be." Fenshaw rested his hand on the smooth metal of the container. "If you knew what was in here, would it make you feel any better?"

"Perhaps." Merrill shrugged. "Does it make any difference?"

"Yes." The thin man poised the sealed box in his hands. "I told you that the Delphi wanted to extend their sphere of knowledge. They cannot travel, personally, I mean. Like plants, they have to stay where they are, but their seeds can travel—and will."

"So that's it." Merrill licked his suddenly dry lips. "That contains the seeds of the Delphi. They want to reach Earth!"

"Yes," said Fenshaw and smiled. "They want to reach Earth—and they will!"

His thin fingers almost caressed the smooth metal.

CHAPTER SIX

Sam stood at the entrance to the spaceport and listened as Merrill gave swift, last-minute instructions.

"Make sure that you hit the right man. He won't know you, but you've got his description. Give the code and he'll pass you through. Got that?"

"Sure." The hunter shrugged with impatience as the old man caught at his arm. "Stop worrying."

"I am worried, Sam. And so should you be. If anything goes wrong..." Merrill bit his lips. "The narcotics, the small cylinder you've got, you will pass on to a man in Luna Station. Get through the customs early and you'll have time for a drink. Go to the Spaceman's Bar, ask for a double Tszenga, and wait. The contact will approach you and you will pass over the cylinder. He will also tell you which landing field is the one for you to land on when you pick Luna-Earth transport. Be guided by him and don't try to be clever. Once you've landed and been cleared, go to the address I told you and pass over the box."

"Then I get the money?"

"That's right. You get the cash and catch the next ship back to Venus." Merrill stared at the hunter. "Don't let me down, Sam."

"I won't." The hunter grinned as the warning siren echoed from the edges of the clearing and rang flatly from the tall buildings. "Goodbye, Merrill. I'll be seeing you." He strode towards the slender spire of the waiting vessel.

Sam wasn't a stranger to space. Before settling down on Venus as a hunter, he had worked a few ships from Earth out to Mars, from Mars towards the asteroids, and had even made one jump to the Jovian System, touching down at Io, Ganymede and Satellite V. A split power pile had almost blinded him and, after he had come out of the hospital, he'd grounded himself. Now, as he climbed the loading ramp, the old magic caught hold of him.

For space was like that. Once a man had ventured out into the void, seen the distant stars burn with all their silent glory against the soft, black velvet of space, felt a touch of the awful grandeur only to be found away from the worlds of men, it was hard to turn back to mundane things. He checked in, passing the usual inspection at the landing ramp, an inspection designed to prevent the carrying of arms, and settled down in his bunk. Space was limited on even the largest vessels, and private cabins were unheard of. Passengers were allocated a bunk and a locker, given regular meals while in transit, rationed with water and forbidden to smoke. The rest of the time they amused themselves, either by drifting in the zero-gravity world of free fall, resting or by playing interminable games of cards.

Sam chose cards.

He was out of his bunk as soon as the pulsing thunder of the rockets had died, recovering with trained swiftness from the acceleration pressure, and the thin, magnetic-backed cards riffled in his hands as he sat, cross-legged, hovering a few inches above the floor.

"How about a game, friends?" He smiled at the other passengers. "Poker? Taro? Name your game and I'm your man."

"May as well." A plump man hooked his leg around a stanchion and squatted down. A thin-faced youngster nodded and joined in. He was followed by a couple more, tourists by their appearance, and the rest of the passengers clustered around the circle, watching the swift interplay of cards and money.

By the time they had reached the braking point, Sam was winning by almost a thousand credits. He grinned as he lay in his bunk feeling the familiar throb of the rockets as they spat their long streamers of speeded ions across the void, and excitement caused a speeding of his heart and a tightness in his chest. He was under no delusions. He knew just what would happen to him if he were caught trying to smuggle narcotics through to Earth, and mentally he adjusted the reward he hoped to get when he handed over the box. He grinned a little wider as he thought of Merrill.

The landing was smooth, handled by an expert, and the faint jar as the wide fins settled on the Luna dust was hardly noticeable. Barely had they landed when the intercom crackled into life and an officer's voice rang through the ship. "Prepare for emergence. We have landed on Luna. All passengers will carry their own possessions. A connecting tube has been fitted and passengers will leave the ship and walk into the customs shed. That is all." The intercom gave a dry click and the passengers began collecting up their gear.

The thin-faced youth pulled at Sam's arm. "Have you been through this before?"

"I have." The hunter stared at the boy. "Why?"

"What's it like?" The youth licked his lips with a nervous gesture. "I mean, are they easy or..."

"Trying to smuggle something?" Sam didn't need an answer; he read the guilt in the youth's eyes. "What is it? Drugs?"

"No. Just a curio I bought for my sister." He looked at Sam. "Are you going to give me away?"

"Why should I?" Sam chuckled and shook his head. "Personally, I wouldn't try it, but I can admire the guts of a man who does." He became serious. "Look. If it isn't much, a doll, say, or an interesting bit of rock, then I'd declare it. They'll confiscate it, of course, but that's about all. If it's anything else..." He shrugged. "Depends on how much the chance is worth to you."

"Plenty," whispered the boy, and sweat shone on his forehead. "I've got to get through."

Sam frowned, staring at the youngster and letting his mind weigh up what he had learned. The boy might be a spy, a plant put among the passengers to watch for contraband, and maybe his confession was just a trick to get him to take him in his confidence. On the other hand, he might be genuine. A lot of people had the bright idea of making expenses by bringing back some contraband and lost their nerve at the last minute. Looking at the sweat beading the young man's face, Sam guessed that he just couldn't afford to lose his nerve.

For a moment he toyed with the idea of letting the youth take the box and cylinder through for him. He could steer him right, give him the code words, and if he were caught... If he were caught, Sam would be caught too. The lad would never stand up beneath a lie detector and he would spill his guts and ruin the entire set-up. Anyway, there just wasn't time.

Slowly Sam walked down the connecting tube from the ship to the great dome of the station, and blinked as he emerged into the glaring lights of the inspection sheds. Passengers milled about the open area, most of them heading towards the line of barred cages behind which waited the customs inspectors. To pass into the station proper, to reach the transit area where the short-shot rockets waited to carry them to Earth, the passengers would have to be cleared. There was no way to avoid it. A speaker began to blare from the roof.

"Passengers for Greater New York, please hurry. Transit rocket will take off within the hour. Passengers for New London. The rocket to England will leave in two hours. Passengers to the Orient. Rocket will leave in three hours."

The speaker clicked into silence and a rush of men and women eager to catch the first rocket almost hid the line of cages. A hand pulled Sam's arm, and he twisted, nerves jumping, to stare into the sweating face of the boy.

"Look, mister," he said eagerly. "I'm a stranger here. If you could help me at all?" He looked hopefully at the hunter.

Sam cursed. "What the hell do you think I am? A tour guide?" He pointed towards the line of cages. "All you have to do is walk into one of those, the inspectors will check you, and then you can be on your way."

"Yes, but...which one?"

Sam almost laughed. He understood what the young man was getting at. Too many people had the idea that an inspector was perfectly willing to let hell and damnation through to Earth provided his palm was well-greased. He grinned as he thought of the young fool pressing a wad of credit notes into an inspector's hand and hoping to be let through without a search. Even if the official had been willing—and there wasn't a chance of that—he wouldn't dare take the money. There were too many electronic eyes watching and pick-up mikes listening to take the certain risk of discovery. On Luna Station, the watchers were as well watched as those they examined.

"I don't know," he said slowly, and smiled as he thought of something. "One's much like another, and you can't bribe any of them; to even try would be asking for a couple of years breaking rocks on Tycho." He narrowed his eyes as he stared at the line of inspectors. "I've got to go now. Be seeing you...I hope." He moved away before the youth could grab his arm.

This was the hard part. Sam felt his stomach tense as he wandered casually about the open area, and his eyes narrowed as he looked from inspector to inspector. It was essential that he pick the right one, and he had to make certain that he was right the first time. Once he entered the cage, there was no way out until he had either been cleared or arrested, and he daren't wait too long; any hesitation would arouse suspicion, and he couldn't chance the slightest touch of doubt.

He felt the first beginnings of panic as he moved slowly down the line.

He couldn't see the contact. The verbal description Merrill had given him didn't seem to fit any of the men behind the wide counter. Medium height, brown hair, brown eyes, sallow complexion, lines running from nose to mouth, odd lobes to his ears and a thin scar just above the left eyebrow. A man like that couldn't be missed and, if he had been there, Sam would have seen him. He swallowed and moved towards the men's room, toying with the desperate idea of dumping the box and cylinder and getting in the clear.

Merrill was a fool! The man could have fallen sick, had his duty roster changed, been fired, fallen dead...anything! It was too slender a chance to rely on and Sam wondered as he thought of the ten years hard labour he would get for attempted smuggling of narcotics.

He turned as he reached the door of the men's room, his eyes flickering as he scanned the men behind the counter in a final desperate search, then paused, a thin smile twisting the corners of his mouth. A fresh face showed behind the counter. A face he knew as well as if he had seen a photograph moved toward the cage.

Deliberately, Sam turned and walked into the rest room. He had headed for that room and he would have to continue the journey. To do otherwise might give grounds for suspicion. He smiled down at the large unavoidable plastic mat lying before him, and deliberately trod firmly on its smooth surface. Hidden cameras photographed him and the camouflaged scale recorded his exact weight. The process would be repeated when he emerged, and cameras would watch him all the time he remained in the room. It wasn't easy to get rid of contraband once it was on the Moon.

Confidently he left the rest room and strode towards the counter. A woman almost beat him to it. A big, over-dressed woman stalking majestically along as if she owned half of Earth and all of the Moon. He slipped into the cage a step ahead of her, smiling as she snorted in disgust at his bad manners and grinned as she slammed the next cage door with unnecessary violence.

He turned to the inspector. "Some people want shooting," he said humorously. "It isn't bad enough that I've had to spend three years, nine months and seven days on a stinking hothouse of a planet, I have to be insulted when I get back home again."

"Anything to declare?" The inspector made no sign that he had recognized the "3-9-7" code signal and for a moment Sam felt panic as he wondered whether or not this was the right man.

He shrugged. "The usual junk." He rummaged in his bag. "A dried fruit; it changes colour in different humidity. A piece of bark. That gash is where a Tryplizard took a swing at me and missed. A tooth from the same Tryp." He spilled articles from his bag. "That's about all."

John nodded, flipping his switches and reading the dials. The man was lying, he knew it, but at the same time he had to admit that it was well done. Even without the code signal, he would have known Sam was a smuggler. The only difference was that, now, he had to pass him through, and do it without any trace of hesitation or apparent collusion. His skin crawled as he remembered the scanning eyes and mechanical ears. He picked up the piece of bark.

"Obviously this hasn't been heat-treated and it will have to be confiscated." He dropped it into the disposal chute. "The same with the fruit." It followed the bark. "The tooth is something else."

"What's the idea?" Sam played his part to perfection. A nice blend of genuine anger and reluctant admission that he was in the wrong. "That tooth's been sterilized. You can see the government seal on the base. Take it easy, will you? Those things have sentimental value."

"Perhaps." John poised the tooth in his hand and examined the seal. He wasn't surprised to find it genuine. He had already located the sealed box. It was disguised as an electronic camera and he had examined it while shielding it from too close a view so that the scanning eyes would only have caught an impression without detail. What else the man might have on him, he didn't know, but suspected a stylo, a bulky pack of playing cards and a pack depilatory tissues.

He passed the tooth beneath the testing plate. "Genuine enough." He threw it back into the bag. "All right, you're clear." He stamped the transit card and pressed the lock release. "Hurry, please. There are others waiting to be examined."

Sam nodded, half-tempted to inform on the young man he had arrived with, then changing his mind as he saw the youth head towards his cage. If the inspector was smart, and somehow Sam knew that he was, he wouldn't need a hint and the more Sam kept his mouth shut, the safer it would be for both of them.

He was sweating with reaction as he headed towards the Spaceman's Bar.

The Tszenga tasted good, sweet with an acid bitterness and cold with foaming effervescence, topped with crushed leaves and heavy with alien odours. He sipped at the tall glass, leaning on the counter and letting his eyes drift over the usual crowd of fresh arrivals, residents and those lucky few who were leaving the Moon for good. A television screen flared with natural colour, the stabbing jets of miniature rocket ships streaming across the void as they strained every plate and seam to reach first place. The voice of the announcer rose with synthetic excitement as he reeled off the numbers and positions of the jet-jockeys and Sam shrugged as he sensed the tension and expectancy of those around him who hoped to win. Draining his glass, he gestured towards the bartender.

"Tszenga, sir?"

"Yes, a double."

Sam took the replenished glass and stared again at the huge screen. The rocket races had given way to a syrup-voiced female wearing a dress which had apparently been sprayed on. She had a face to match. Sam was just getting around to the point of wondering how the hell she ever got undressed for bed when a hand touched his arm.

"Pardon me," murmured a low voice. "Would I be wrong if I suggested that you have just arrived from Venus?"

"No." Sam twisted on his stool and stared at the small, smoothly dressed man.

"How long did you stay?"

"Three years, nine months, seven days." Sam took a gulp at his drink. "Why?"

"Nothing special." The stranger smiled. "I understand that Venus is a hot planet. If you would join me...?"

"Thanks." Sam drained his glass. "I'll have a Tszenga. A double." He stared at the man. "Perhaps you could advise me. I want to get to Earth and I'm not sure which would be the best landing field to make for. Have you any suggestions?"

"Perhaps."

Sam grunted and took the stylo from his pocket. He held it a moment, then, setting it down, found a scrap of paper. "If you'll just write down the address...?"

"Greater New York is very efficient," murmured the stranger. He scribbled on the paper and slipped the stylo in his own pocket. It was done with a deceptive casualness, the sort of thing which happens every day, and Sam admired the man for his quick understanding. "New London is as bad. Both spaceports vie with each other to see which can find the most contraband. A laudable pursuit, but irritating to one who has travelled far and is in a hurry to reach home." He frowned. "I would suggest Glynod. The rocket leaves within the hour and you could catch the stratoliner to either America or England."

"Thanks." Sam lifted his drink.

"Is there anything else?"

"Nothing."

The stranger nodded, losing himself in the crowd. Sam didn't look after him.

CHAPTER SEVEN

Glynod was the Central European spaceport serving the continent and the west of Russia. Traffic to it was brief, most people preferring to land at New London and continue their journey by stratoliner or monorail. Mostly it was used for freight and, inevitably, the passenger inspection tended to be careless.

Sam stood in line as an official examined and stamped transit cards and identification papers. He stared at the great tooth, grunted as he saw the government seal, touched the shell of the electronic camera and passed Sam out into the embarkation hall. The hunter wasted no time. A heliojet took him a hundred kilometres and dropped him at a monorail station, where he caught the train for Paris. There he booked a seat in the Transatlantic stratoliner and arrived at Greater New York three hours after leaving the French capital. A turbo-cab took him to the outskirts of the city and a second dropped him outside a small hotel.

The receptionist, a faded woman who still tried to retain a semblance of youth, smiled at him as she pushed forward the guest register. "You wish a room, sir?"

"Yes." Sam showed his identity papers and scrawled his signature in the book. "Have you videophone service?"

"Certainly, Mr. Steel. You wish to make a call?"

"Later." Sam rubbed the stubble on his chin. "First, I want a bath, a meal and some information." He smiled at her. "The last two I get for myself. You can connect the videophone to my room." He was gone before she could smile again.

The bath was good, the light-shower even better and, as Sam wiped off his stubble with depilatory tissue, he felt himself relax for the first time since arriving on the Moon. He smiled towards the disguised box lying on his bed. All he had to do now was to collect the money and... He smiled again as he thought of Merrill waiting more than thirty-five million miles away, and smiled even wider as he picked up the bulky pack of playing cards and the packet of tissue. Both contained narcotics. Either would bring in a cool ten thousand if he could find the right buyer and that, together with the money he would collect for the box, would set him up for life.

A hum came from the cabinet in the corner and he crossed the room with long strides, sitting on the stool and staring at the videophone screen.

"Your call, sir." The operator's voice sounded coolly remote. Shall I cut in visual?"

"Yes." Sam stared at the blank surface of the screen. It writhed, flushing with a wash of rainbow colours, then steadied into the head and shoulder image of a young, neatly uniformed girl. "Connect." Sam leaned forward as the image dissolved and gave way to another.

A man stared at him from the screen.

A round-faced, swollen-necked man. A hard-eyed, thin-mouthed man. A man who had looked on too much suffering and dipped his fingers in too much filth. A man who was consumed by an ideal, a would-be dictator. Arrogant, cruel, utterly selfish and wholly untrustworthy. Sam stared at the image, feeling the other's eyes rove over his features and, automatically, he leaned far back in his chair.

"Stay as you are," said the man quietly, and his voice was a feral purr. "You have moved out of focus."

"Scrambler setting?" Sam rested his finger over the dial. "May I suggest 397."

"Make it 39739."

Sam nodded and began to spin the dial. The setting would break up his transmitted image and voice into an unrecognisable jumble of electronic impulses which could only be sorted and restored to their original by a companion machine in the other cabinet. The scrambler system made for utter secrecy, for it was impossible to tune in on any conversation unless the setting was known. With a five-figure dial, the possible number of settings was one hundred thousand and it would take hours to try them all.

The image on the screen wavered a little, blurred, then steadied as the twin instruments synchronised to the altered wave pattern. For a moment, the two men stared at each other in silence, watchful, wary, each waiting for the other to speak.

Sam broke the silence. "There was a name," he murmured. "A friend of mine on Venus told me to ask for it."

"Stephan." The image nodded and something like a smile touched the hard mouth. "You have it?"

"Perhaps."

"Perhaps what?" Irritation sharpened the purring voice. "I suggest we dispense with this nonsense. Do you have it or not?"

"Nonsense you call it?" Sam thinned his lips in seething anger. "Damn it, man! I've been on hooks ever since I left Venus and I've just about had enough of it. I've got what I'm supposed to have. Have you got your end of the bargain?"

"The money?"

"Of course! What else do you think I want?"

"I shall send a man to collect the box," said Stephan evenly. "The money will be sent you as soon as I have checked the contents."

"No."

"No?"

"Not on your life. You bring the money and we'll make an even swap."

"I see. You are suspicious. Perhaps I shouldn't blame you for that." Secret amusement shook the fat figure. "I will bring you the money. I have the address of your hotel and will arrive at midnight. I trust that is satisfactory?"

"I'll tell you when I count the cash." Sam put out a hand and touched the switch. "One other thing, Stephan."

"Yes?"

"Come alone." He threw the contact and the screen blurred into milky whiteness, the scrambler automatically returning to the open channel, and the dull light behind the scanning eyes died to a red glow and then faded as the pulsing current ceased to flow.

For a long moment Sam sat in the cubicle frowning, his mind busy with thoughts.

Leaving the cabinet, he picked up the box from where it lay on the bed, snapped the catches of the camera shell, and let the sealed container fall out onto the palm of his hand. For the hundredth time, he wondered just what it contained, half-tempted to open it and, remembering Merrill's warning, half-afraid to touch it.

He stared at it, remembering the hard bleakness of Stephan's eyes, the feral purr of his voice, and he smiled as he stared at the enigmatic container.

From the hotel, he went to a nearby restaurant, enjoying good food well-cooked, savouring spiced wine and listening to genuine music as compared to the canned and recorded stuff sent to Venus. A city directory guided him to the next place, a tall, frowning structure of concrete and steel with a single high door guarded by armed men in uniform. He strode past them, the box hidden beneath his short jacket and, before they could decide whether or not to stop him, he was talking to a poker-faced man sitting behind a grilled window.

"I want a safety deposit box."

"Yes, sir. Key or electronic?"

"Electronic."

"Yes, sir. For how long?"

"A week, maybe longer. Is that possible?"

"Certainly. If you will leave rental for one month, a rebate will be given for each unused week of the period." The man snapped his fingers towards a guard. "Number Five will attend to you, sir." He hesitated. "The rental?"

Sam peeled bills from his roll and followed the guard along a corridor, down a flight of steps, along another echoing tunnel and into a small room covered with the blank faces of electronically operated safety deposit boxes.

The guard pointed towards them. "Number 765, sir. Just place your hand on the plate and the pattern will be recorded."

He stepped out of the room and Sam rested his hand against the dull metal of the scanning surface. Hidden machinery whined, something clicked and a long, deep drawer slid from the wall. Placing the box within the drawer, he slammed it, rested his palm against the plate again and smiled as the drawer slid open. Closing it again, he followed the guard.

"What if I forget my number?"

"It is on file at the front office, sir, as no one but yourself can open the box if it isn't really important."

"I see. Is there any other way to open the box other than my palm-print?"

"No, sir."

Sam grunted, knowing that the man was lying. It was obvious that there would be a master pattern keyed to each lock, but he didn't argue. The box was as safe as it could ever be, and he breathed a lot easier as he left the building. Outside, he deliberately tore his receipt into fragments, scattering them in the faint breeze, and smiled as the wind caught them and swirled them away.

From the depository, he caught a turbo-cab to the poorer section of the city and walked about until he found a small, dingy shop. Once an ancient sign had swung on a rusted bracket, and though it had long since been torn down, yet there was no mistaking what the shop was. Even in a modern age, people still found it essential to raise money on their possessions, and the dingy window was filled with garish jewellery, chronometers, broken instruments and the general rubbish accumulated over many years.

A bell jangled as Sam pushed open the door and a man, blinking like some awakened owl, moved slowly towards the scarred counter.

"Yes?"

"I want a gun," said Sam with direct abruptness. "What have you got for sale?"

"For sale?" The man gestured at the cluttered shelves. "There are many things here for sale, but a gun? No."

"A pity." Sam leaned against the counter and idly flipped his roll of credit notes. "I only want a gun." He stared at the owl-like man. "I'm willing to pay for it. Well?"

"Police?"

"I'm no informer and I'm not wanted." Sam peeled off some of the notes. "I've got a bad memory, too. When I leave this place, I'll forget all about it." He half-moved towards the door. "If you haven't what I want, then I'll try somewhere else."

"Wait." The pawnbroker nervously licked his lips. "Why don't you go to a gunsmith?"

"Because I don't want to register for a license." Sam returned to the counter. "Well? Have you got a gun or haven't you?"

The pawnbroker had. It was a small, flat, sinister-looking needler, the anaesthetic darts capable of penetrating normal clothing at twenty feet. It was a short-range weapon, silent and handy in a crowd, a favourite of the hoodlums and hold-up men for its swift efficiency.

Sam took it, paying three times the normal cost and buying a box of ammunition to complete the deal. He wasn't wholly satisfied, a high-velocity pistol would have been better, even an old-fashioned automatic, but he had to take what he could get, and the chance of a stranger being able to pick up an unlicensed gun at short notice was remote.

Loading the weapon, he left the shop and stopped by at a Protection Office.

"I want a bodyguard, armed. The best you have."

"Yes, sir." The girl receptionist didn't show surprise. "What duties?"

"I want him to wait outside and watch to see that certain parties don't remove me by force." Sam gave his hotel address. The girl took his particulars, asked him to wait in an anteroom, and when she finally called him, he knew that the selected bodyguard had memorised every detail of his face and build.

The girl looked down at a large-scale map. "The house you mention has two entrances, the main one and a service door at the rear. I suggest that the Protection Officer be stationed within the building."

"Make it two instead of one." Sam counted out money. "I want protection from nine until dawn. It may not be necessary, but I want the men in position all the time. I can rely on you?"

"Certainly, sir." The girl didn't ask questions and Sam didn't volunteer any answers. With the terrible overcrowding of modern cities and the limitations of the police forces, the private guards—or Protection Officers, as they called themselves—had become a part the normal way of life. They could be hired by the hour, the day, the week or for any period during which extra protection was considered necessary. They were armed and they would shoot to protect their clients. Any lawsuits following were the responsibility of the client; the guards merely acted as his agents.

It was almost nine when Sam returned to his hotel room. He had eaten, gone to a sensatape show and drunk a little more than was good for him. He staggered a little as he entered the hotel, grinned at the porter who helped him in and out of the lift, waited while the man opened his door, and almost fell into the room.

Stephan was waiting for him.

The fat man sat in a chair, his feet on a stool, the dull metal of a weapon glinting in his hand. He smiled, catlike, without humour, and his feral voice sobered the hunter with its quiet menace.

"The box, Steel. Where is it?"

"Box?" Sam blinked and grunted as he slumped into a chair. From a pocket, he took a package of cigarettes, shook one out, puffed it to glowing life, and stared at the fat man through a veil of drifting smoke. "I didn't expect you until midnight."

"I decided to come early." The gun moved in the big hand and Stephan brought down his feet and twisted a little in his chair. "I do not intend wasting time, Steel. Where is the box?"

"Where is the money?"

"You will be paid...after I have the box."

"I see." Sam dragged smoke down into his lungs. "So we can't trust each other, is that it?" He gave a mirthless smile. "Funny. I bring the box all the way from Venus, look you up, and you still can't trust me. You fool! If I'd wanted to cross you, would I have even bothered to contact you? Use your head, Stephan. Get rid of some of that dictator-complex and start thinking like a rational being."

For a moment he thought that the fat man would strike him and tensed, his fingers poised around the cigarette, ready to flip it into the hard eyes, his feet pressing down on to the carpet, ready to hurl him away from the menace of the pistol. For a long moment the tension held, then, surprisingly, the fat man shrugged and slipped the pistol into an underarm holster.

"You are a brave man, Steel, or a foolish one. Only time will tell." His thick fingers pulled a wallet from beneath his jacket. "You want money? Here." He tossed a sheaf of bills towards the hunter. Now, where is the box?"

"Wait a minute." Sam riffled the money. "Where's the rest?"

"I am attending to that. That money in your hand is for your trouble. Give me the box, please."

"Like hell!" Sam tossed the sheaf of money onto the bed. You think that you can pay me off like that? Damn it! That isn't a fifth of what I was promised. I'm damned if you get the box until I get my money. All of it. Merrill's, too. Now give, or you'll never get what you're after."

"No?"

"No." Something warned the hunter. It may have been a shadow—if shadows could exist in a shadowless room—or it may have been the reflection of something behind him shown in the fat man's eyes. Whatever it was, it brought swift action and, even as the club swung towards his head, he was moving, throwing himself down towards the carpet, his hand clawing at the needler in his pocket.

A man stood above him, the loaded club still in his hand and his eyes, as the tiny dart struck him, held a shocked surprise. For a moment he seemed to waver, to sway as a tree sways in a high wind, then, slowly, buckling at the knees and collapsing at the hip, he fell towards the floor. The sound of his face hitting the carpet made a hollow echo in the soundproof room.

Before he had touched the floor, Sam had twisted, jerked to his feet with an incredible burst of energy, and recovered his advantage. He smiled as he dug the muzzle of the needler into soft flesh.

"Still want to play this game, Fatso?" The gun dug harder. "I expected this. You're the kind of man who'd think it smart to work the good old double-cross. It shows just what kind of fool you really are."

"Remove your pistol, please." Incredibly Stephan betrayed no emotion and his eyes, as he stared at the unconscious man on the floor, held a cold hostility. "It is time we stopped being clever with each other and got to the point."

"I agree." Sam lifted the fat man's weapon from its concealed holster and dropped it into his pocket. Still holding the needler, he sat down, lit a fresh cigarette and grinned through the coiling blue smoke. "Shall we start with the money?"

"If you wish." Stephan frowned a little as a wreath of smoke coiled about his face. "First, let me apologize for what just happened. It was a mistake and the fool deserved all you did to him." Coldly, he leaned forward and spurned the silent figure with the toe of his shoe. "Second, about the money." He stared at Sam. "I don't know what you may have heard or what you expect, but I am going to put it to you as an intelligent man. Would you rather accept what I offered, give me the box, and be free of all worry, or would you prefer to die?" He spread his hands. "It's as simple as that."

"Not quite." Sam breathed smoke and spoke around his cigarette. "You haven't got the box yet."

"No, but we will."

"Perhaps." Something in his tone brought the fat man upright on the edge of the chair.

"You have it? It is safe? Quick, you fool, tell me!"

"It is safe—for the time being."

"Then we will find it. You will tell us where it is."

Stephan spoke with a childish conviction which almost made the hunter laugh. He leaned down, one hand resting lightly on the pistol and, as he looked at the fat man, anger surged through him, bringing the hot blood pounding at his temples and making the flagrant smoke of the cigarette taste dry and bitter.

"What manner of fool are you, Stephan? Why are you trying to operate out of your class?" He crushed out the cigarette with savage force. "Here we are, all of us, sitting as pretty as any men could wish, and you spoil it all by trying to act like a third-rate crook. Man, don't you realize the possibilities? We've a pipeline straight to Venus, the inspection fixed and the contacts made. We could make a fortune every trip, flood the market with narcotics, make enough to keep us in style for a thousand years. There's no limit to what we could do. I passed and so could others. It's the chance of a lifetime, and you're throwing it all away by arguing over a few lousy credits. Hell! If you can't handle it, I'll find someone who can."

"Wait!" Stephan half-rose from his chair then slumped down again as Sam picked up the needler. "Half of what you say is correct. I don't have the money to pay you, not yet, but I shall have soon."

"How soon?"

"Within a few weeks after you give me the box."

"You mean after you sell the stuff?" Sam shook his head. My terms are strictly C.O.D."

"But you don't understand." The fat man's voice held a strained desperation. "I know that the box isn't here. We searched the place before you arrived and, unless I find it, I'll be ruined. You'll get your money, Steel, every credit of it, but you'll have to trust me for a while."

"Why should I? With the pipeline through to Venus, I can collect any time I want to."

"Don't talk like a fool." The fat man dabbed at his glistening forehead. "How long do you think the inspector will remain fixed? How long will it be before they switch schedules and your carrier misses his contact? A trick like that can only work once, twice at the best, then something will trip us all up." He swallowed. "Mine is a better way."

"Yes?"

"Do you know what is in that box?"

"Narcotics. Why?"

"Why?" Stephan shrugged. "Nothing, or perhaps you're just being careful. The contents of that box are worth millions, billions if handled right. I've got the set-up to handle it. I can pay everyone every credit I've promised but I can't do it straight away."

"Why not?" Sam frowned at the fat man. He didn't like the way things were going. He had the impression that Stephan was talking merely to gain time. He glanced down at the man lying at his feet and deliberately fired another dart into the soft flesh of his upper arm. "What's all the mystery about?"

"The contents of that box are seeds, Steel. Now do you get it? Seeds from Venus. Mutated seeds which will grow on Earth!"

"Grow?" Slowly understanding came to the hunter and he stared at the fat man with new respect. Seeds from Venus just didn't grow on Earth, not unless they had special conditions and certain rare metals were provided in their soil. Spores would grow. Spores would spread and increase with frightening speed. The great fruit panic had been directly caused by Venusian spores attacking the soft fruit blossoms and ruining the crop, but no Venusian seed had ever been known to grow and breed true.

And the narcotic plants were seed-grown.

He smiled at the thought of it. A constant source of Tszenga dust, at five hundred credits a pinch. Or perhaps it was Phelihan juice, one drop of which could accelerate the normal metabolism and sense so that, to the user, all others moved at a snail's pace. Athletes would be willing to pay highly for Phelihan.

It would literally be a golden harvest—and he was the man who could obtain the precious box.

CHAPTER EIGHT

The plant was something like a cactus, with the same thick, fleshy leaves, covered with cruel spines and hooked thorns. The leaves sprang from a rounded bole, each as high as a man's waist, and were slightly concave on their inner surfaces. It stood in a pot on the floor of the concealed room and, as Fenshaw passed by, the leaves quivered a little as if preparing to snap together. The thin man smiled as he noticed the motion.

He paused, picked up a slender rod, and carefully touched the inner surface of one of the leaves. Immediately they snapped together, the hooked spines driving forward like daggers, the entire plant locking itself into a tight, unbroken mass about the rod. The scientist tugged it away, stared down at the plant for a moment, then turned to examine a bulbous growth within a sealed container. He looked up as Merrill entered by the concealed panel.

The old man seemed torn by a conflict of opposed emotions. His sunken eyes burned within their deep sockets and, as he dragged his twisted leg behind him, he reminded the other man of some half-crushed insect crawling across the floor. Tiredly he slumped into a chair and shuddered a little as he saw the slowly opening leaves of the cactus-like plant.

"Been playing again, Fenshaw?"

"I have been testing the reflexes of the plant, if that's what you mean." Fenshaw stared at the growth within the sealed container and swung a powerful magnifier towards him. "You want to see me?"

"Yes."

"A moment." The thin man pursed his lips as he stared at the magnified image of the bulbous fungi-like growth. He nodded as if satisfied, swung back the magnifier and sat opposite the old man. "What is it?"

"You know what it is, Fenshaw. It's been weeks since Sam took the box to Earth. When am I going to get my reward?"

"As soon as the Delphi are satisfied that their seeds have been planted and that the new organism has taken root." He shrugged. "It will take a little time. After all, interplanetary telepathy isn't possible to a seed or a new shoot. We shall have to wait until the plants are mature."

"That's not what you said before."

"Isn't it?" Fenshaw didn't look at the old man. "I would have thought that was obvious."

"You promised that as soon as the box had been delivered the Delphi would carry out their promise." Merrill stared down at his withered hands. "I'm an old man, Fenshaw. I can't afford to wait much longer."

"I'm afraid that you will have to." There was a casual indifference in the thin man's voice, a careless disregard for others and, hearing it, Merrill shifted uneasily in his chair.

"Sam may have been caught," he muttered. "The box may have been confiscated and destroyed."

"The box arrived safely."

"How do you know?"

Fenshaw smiled, a thin, bleak smile, utterly devoid of humour and, behind his thick lenses, his eyes held an abysmal contempt. He didn't answer the question, but, as he sat, his eyes roved constantly over the assembled plants and containers.

"I asked you a question, Fenshaw!" Something of the old man's youth returned as he spoke and his voice cracked in the silence of the room like the lash of a whip. "I'll have you remember who is the boss here. I want to know."

"Know what?"

"Are you in communication with Earth?"

"Perhaps." Again the thin man's eyes drifted over the exotic plants. He seemed to be utterly bored by the old man's presence.

Merrill thinned his lips and, as he leaned forward, his withered hands trembled as they rested on his knees. "I don't like your attitude, Fenshaw. Now, for the last time, have you received information from Earth that the box arrived?"

"Yes."

"Good. Then we have done our part and you can tell the Delphi we want our reward. Their seeds have been planted and there is no more we can do." He stared at the thin man. "You will tell them that, Fenshaw?"

"Perhaps." Again the weak eyes drifted over the plants and the cold voice held the same indifference. "If you are finished, Merrill, there is some work I have to do."

"Damn your work!" Anger thickened the dry, rustling tones. "I want a straight answer to a straight question. When do I get what's due to me?"

"I've told you. When the seeds have grown and telepathic communication has been established between Earth and Venus."

"And how long will that take?"

"A year, perhaps." Fenshaw shrugged. "Maybe two. Does it matter?"

"A year!" Merrill sagged back in his chair. "You are joking."

"I am not a humorous man, Merrill." For the first time, Fenshaw stared into the sunken eyes and, behind his thick lenses, his eyes held a secret, sardonic amusement. "After all, what is a year when compared with restored youth? You have waited a long time, old man. You can wait a little longer."

"Can I?" Merrill started down at his withered hands. "Thank you for reminding me that I am old," he said quietly. "An old man has nothing to lose." He stared at Fenshaw. "Unless I get the promised rejuvenation treatment, and get it soon, I shall contact the Space Guard and inform them that Venusian seeds have been smuggled to Earth. I shall tell them everything. I may be a fool. Perhaps I am, but even a fool can be dangerous." He looked down at his hands again. "There it is, Fenshaw. Either the Delphi carry out their part of the bargain or their seeds shall be found and destroyed."

"Will they?" Fenshaw's cold voice held a brittle amusement. "And where will they look for the seeds? Earth is a big place, don't forget, and they could be anywhere by this time. No, Merrill, your threats do not frighten me."

"They will arrest you, Fenshaw. I suggest that you contact the Delphi and tell them of my ultimatum." His voice became almost pleading. "After all, what do I ask? Only the very thing they promised me at the beginning of all this. They can't let me down now."

"You will have to wait, Merrill. There is nothing else you can do."

"I can contact the Space Guard," reminded the old man. "I haven't been so trusting as you imagine. Even though the Earth is large, an organized search could find the box, and I have a shrewd idea just where he would be." Merrill leaned back in his chair. "I'm too old not to take elementary precautions, Fenshaw. I had the box in my possession for quite some time and I took the chance to impregnate the outer covering with one of our synthetic radioactives. It won't show on normal instruments, but the Guard could track it down with our tracer equipment. And once they find the box, they will find your mysterious friends who have promised to tell them approximately where to look for it." He smiled. "I think that the Delphi will agree that I have earned my reward. The alternative is the complete destruction of their plans."

"You swine!" Fenshaw half-rose from his seat and his thin lip showed stained teeth in a tiger-snarl. "You seek to threaten me!"

"Not you, Fenshaw. The Delphi."

"The Delphi?" Fenshaw relaxed and suddenly his thin shoulders were shaking with inward laughter. "Of course. I forgot The Delphi!" He chuckled and Merrill felt the touch of something strange and menacing as he looked at the scientist.

"Yes, the Delphi. What's so funny about that?"

"Nothing." Fenshaw tried to control his laughter and couldn't. "The Delphi! A planet-wide intelligence! Plant gods! Really, Merrill, how stupid can you get?"

"Stupid?" The old man frowned. "I don't understand."

"Words." Fenshaw wiped the thick lenses of his spectacles. "The most potent force known to man. Words to describe something which doesn't exist. Words to play on an old man's fears and hopes and dreams. Cunning words to veil lies and deceit. Empty words, Merrill. Empty words."

"You lied!" The dry voice seemed to choke with sudden understanding. "You made a fool out of me."

"You made a fool out of yourself, Merrill. You and all the others I have used." Abruptly Fenshaw lost his amusement and the contempt dripping from his voice made the old man seethe with helpless shame. "Did you really think that your youth could be restored? A moment's calm thinking would have convinced you otherwise. Even if the Delphi—a nice name, that, don't you think?—were the repositories of the intelligence I claimed them to be, still they could never take your twisted body and make it whole again. Your chemistry is too alien for any plant to understand. There would need to be years of research, of experiment, and you imagined that they could take you, adjust your metabolism, and give you a completely new body. You are the fool, Merrill, not I."

"Then..."

"I used you," Fenshaw interrupted. "I used you as I used Sam, used those two fools of swamp-rats, as I am using the man on Earth." He smiled. "It is so easy to use men. All that is necessary is to find out their weaknesses, to play on their dreams and to promise the universe. Youth, the eternal desire to start again, that was your weakness and you lost all shrewdness, all cunning when blinded by that golden promise. Of all men, your sort is the easiest to delude. You want to believe so strongly that you are easy prey for anyone who will tell you the words which you want to hear. You ask no questions, you take everything on faith, and so great is your fear of losing what you have never really had, that you blind yourselves to the truth. I guessed your weakness, Merrill, as soon as I saw your twisted body."

"Yes," muttered the old man sickly. "I wanted to believe." He looked at his withered hands and distorted limbs. "I wanted it so much."

"Sam is normal," said Fenshaw, speaking more to himself than to the old man sitting crumpled in the chair. "By that I mean his God is money and he will do anything to obtain it. Most men are like that. They can delude themselves, find justification for what they do, but their motivation is the simple one of pure greed. I had no trouble with Sam."

"And the others? The man on Earth?"

"Power. He is a would-be dictator and suffers from delusions of grandeur. He is not concerned with how he obtains his power, an empire of drug addicts would be as welcome to him as any other form of servile obedience. He will be happy only as long as men and women obey his commands—and he will do anything to obtain that power." Fenshaw almost spat in his contempt. "Men! Animals with animal motivations! They deliberately ruin their own civilisation for the sake of personal desires. They deserve to die."

Something in the thin voice, the naked fire smouldering in the weak eyes, the tenseness of the scrawny body made Merrill stare at the scientist with startled understanding. He blinked, forcing himself to remain seated, but his thin, claw-like hand twitched and twitched again as it moved, insect-like towards his pocket. "The box," he muttered, and nervously licked his dry lips. "Why have those men collect it from the valley?"

"Would you have believed in the Delphi if I hadn't?" Fenshaw shrugged, not aware of the way his tongue was running away with his secrets or, if aware, not caring. "I was in the valley when they arrived. You may have noticed one of the jetcopters disappeared about that time. I filled the box and sealed it and I watched that big fool tremble with fear and superstitious dread as he collected it. It was essential that they should do what they did. I wanted no trail leading to me in case of trouble."

"I see." Merrill felt physically ill as he realised how the thin man had deluded them all. "And, of course, they had to die. As Sam has to die. And the man on Earth?"

"He will die also."

"Naturally." Merrill was bitter. "What is one life, more or less, to you?"

"Nothing." There was something about the way he said it, a peculiar intonation of the word, which sent the skin crawling with primitive warning between the old man's shoulder blades.

"Nothing," repeated the scientist. "Nothing! They are all dirt, all of them, scum crawling over the surface of the world, and the sooner they are dead, the better. All of them! All!" He glared at Merrill and tiny spots of foam edged the corners of his writhing mouth. "I hate them! I hate them all!"

"You're insane!" The old man cringed in his chair and his thin hand moved faster towards his sagging pocket. "Out of your mind. What do you have to gain by all this?"

"Gain?" Scorn edged the rising voice. "You think that I want money? You think that I'm like all the rest of the two-legged animals? I don't want money. All I want is to see the crawling scum of civilisation, of humanity, of the things which are men, wiped from the face of the planets. I want to see an end of killing and greed, of burning and destroying, of exploitation and hypocrisy. Kill them all! Wipe the slate clean so that some other race, as yet unknown, can build where the monkey-men have been torn down."

Fenshaw paused, his eyes wild and his thin chest heaving with emotion. Watching him, Merrill realised that the man's control had finally slipped and that he faced a madman with a madman's insane strength. His hand hitched towards his pocket, the thumb slid over the edge, the rest of his fingers bent to follow.

"I have suffered too much at the hands of men." Fenshaw stared sombrely at the assembled plants. "They laughed at me, scorned me, robbed me of my rightful heritage. I came to Venus to escape from them, and here I found the same old conditions. Men intent only on seeing how much they could rip from the guts of the new world. Exploiters, slashing down the trees, ripping up the top-soil with their open-cast mines, ruining the delicate balance of life with their insane hunting and searches for rare plants. How long will it be, Merrill, before Venus becomes a second Earth? How long before the jazz and the drugs, the drink and the commercials have turned this paradise into purgatory? I won't let it happen,

Merrill. I shall stop it, have stopped it, and Mankind will become an unclean memory!"

Paranoia. A deep-rooted persecution complex coupled with suicidal tendencies. Merrill could recognise the sickness as he stared at the sweating scientist. Hate. Sheer naked hate against all things and everyone. It wasn't enough that Fenshaw should kill himself, he had to take everyone along with him, and the old man wondered at the diabolical cunning of the madman in plotting so deeply and so... He swallowed as his fingers closed around the butt of the high-velocity pistol in his pocket.

"What was in that box, Fenshaw?"

"The box?" The thin man smiled. "Pandora's box? Guess."

"I can't guess. Tell me."

"Pandora's box held all the ills of man, and when it was opened nothing was left inside but hope." Fenshaw giggled. "I have done better than that, for in my box is the death of Earth and there is no hope." He giggled again then, before Merrill could guess what he was about to do, had flung himself forward, one hand snatching at the thin wrist, the other tearing the pistol away from the weak grasp. "You underrate me, Merrill. Did you think that I would permit you to kill me?"

"What is in that box?"

"Death." Fenshaw smiled as he tossed the flat pistol on his palm. "Death for every man, woman and child." His smile became wider. "I shall have a sweet revenge and, when they are dying, they shall have cause to remember me."

"But how, Fenshaw? How?"

"The true scientific spirit." The scientist nodded and tossed the gun onto a bench. "Even death cannot turn you from your purpose. You still display curiosity. A pity that you will never live to inform anyone of what you are about to learn." He chuckled as if at a huge joke. "I'm going to kill you, Merrill. You know that, don't you?"

"Why?" Merrill wiped sweat from his streaming features. "Why should you kill me? I've helped you, been your friend. I even saved your life and found you a job. Why should you kill a helpless old man?"

"You know too much, and you will soon know more." Fenshaw sighed. "It has been such a relief to talk to you like this. At times, the strain of pretence was almost more than I could bear, the urge to shout out my hatred, to see their stupid faces alter when they knew what I had discovered..." He shrugged. "Never mind. The results are worth every moment of it." He stared at Merrill. "Surely you see that I must kill you? I cannot trust you to keep silent and that trick with the synthetic radioactive tracer element..." He shook his head. "Not that it will make any difference, of course, but it would be foolish to take risks."

"What is in the box, Fenshaw?"

"Yes, the box. You are interested, I believe." The scientist rose and walked over to where the bulbous growth showed like yellow-white balloon beneath the transparent plastic of its cover. "You are familiar with spores, Merrill? I see that you are. You must also be familiar with parasitical fungi. You know that most species have extremely rapid growth and, if conditions are right, can grow, spore and collapse within an incredibly short space of time." His thin hand was caressing as he touched the cover. "This is a mutated specimen of a rather special fungus I have developed. Incidentally, the oxygen content within this container is very low and the pressure is not more than eight ounces to the square inch. There is a reason for this."

Despite himself, Merrill was interested and he rose from the chair and leaned towards the container.

Fenshaw gestured proudly towards the growth. "Now. I will bleed in a little air, raise the pressure to two pounds an inch and thus increase the oxygen content." His thin fingers rested on a valve. "Watch closely. I cannot repeat the demonstration." He twisted the valve.

For a second, nothing seemed to happen. The slight hissing of the air as it rushed into the near-vacuum died as Fenshaw closed the valve, then...

The fungus exploded into tremendous growth. It swelled like an inflated balloon, expanding with a horrible swirling motion of its outer skin, pressing against the plastic and seeming to strain against the clear walls.

"Quickly now, before it breaks free." Fenshaw's voice was tense with excitement. "Notice the spore cups on the outer skin. Notice the texture and the grasping root-tendrils. See how the emitted acid fogs the plastic." He thumbed a button and fire crackled within the container, blue electric fire searing into the swollen growth and reducing it to a heap of ash. "It would be unwise to let the internal pressure build too high. If it ever got free..." He let his voice fade into silence as he stared at the now-empty container.

"What was it?" Merrill found himself trembling as he thought of the savage violence of the incredible growth. "A fungus, I know, but the growth! How did you do it?"

"Mutation. Selection. Inbreeding and environmental control. The fertility of the spores is over ninety percent. The life cycle is one day. The resistance is on a level with that of bacteria. The aggressiveness is high. They are parasitic, of course, and with normal air pressure and oxygen content the growth of a single spore would fill this room. Each growth will, after twenty-four hours, emit several million spores and each spore is so small and light that they will hover like a dust mote in the air. They could lie dormant for a million years and spring to life immediately when they came in contact with a suitable host." Fenshaw smiled. "Pandora's Box."

"Is that what you have sent to Earth?" Sick realization of what the madman had done gripped the old man's heart. "A box full of spores from that thing? Why, you fool, if ever they are released..."

"It will be the end of civilization," said Fenshaw calmly. They will grow and spread, spread and grow until not a single living thing is to be found on the entire planet. They will be carried as dust in the spaceships and Mars and Mercury, Venus and the Jovian moons will all be washed clean of the filth of humanity." Spittle drooled from the writhing lips. "You have seen how a spore-trap works. Imagine Earth covered with them, each a million times more virulent than any previously known. Once the box is open, they will explode outwards in a cloud which nothing can stop. It will be the end of Earth, Merrill. The end of Humanity."

"You're insane! No one would open the box knowing what's inside."

"But Stephan doesn't know what is inside. The fool believes that it contains seeds from which he can grow an endless supply of narcotics. He has the combination of the electronic lock and he will be among the first to die." Fenshaw smiled. Then, with startling abruptness, his eyes changed, altered their expression, and Merrill felt the touch of sheer terror as he stared at the madman.

"Now you must die," whispered the thin man, and his hands were claws as he lunged forward.

Panic gave the old man strength. He twisted, kicking out with a feeble foot and, twisting, he threw himself towards the high-velocity pistol lying on the bench where Fenshaw had thrown it. The smooth metal felt slippery to his grasp, the trigger almost too hard to pull and, as he struggled to level the weapon, Fenshaw dived at his feet.

Merrill fired as he went down, clamping down hard on the trigger and sending a stream of the tiny, incredibly fast slugs whining across the room. Containers smashed and the reek of spilled sap from exotic plants and bottled specimens filled the air. Fenshaw snarled like an animal as he clawed at the weapon, the tiny slugs exploding into incandescence as they struck the walls, the tremendous kinetic energy converted into heat as they slammed against the unyielding surface.

The old man sobbed as he felt the pistol torn from his weak grasp. Above him, Fenshaw showed stained teeth in a grin of triumph and his hands, as they closed around Merrill's thin throat, felt like metal claws.

"You're going to die, you swine! Die like all the rest of the scum. Die!" His hooked fingers dug deep into the soft flesh of the old man's neck.

Desperation made Merrill do what he did. He was dying, he knew it, and knew, too, that if he surrendered to the roaring tides of blackness surging all around him, Earth would die with him.

Grimly he lifted his right arm, poised it and drove the stiffened fingers directly into the hate-filled eyes glaring down at him.

Fenshaw screamed.

He shrieked with the pain from his injured eyes, throwing himself back and away from the old man, blood and tears streaming from between the shielding fingers.

Back he went.

Back; the sound of his screams dull against the soundproofed walls, his legs threshing wildly as he kicked himself away from the man who had injured him.

Back to where a tall plant like a spined cactus waited with open leaves.

He touched the concave inner surface.

He screamed once as the leaves snapped shut around his head and face. A shriek of utter fear and pain, then, as spines drove like hooked daggers into his brain, merciful silence closed about him.

For a while he threshed, his long legs twitching in reflex action as they tried to free his head from the locked plant, then he sagged, relaxing and looking like a thing of rag and straw.

Slowly, from between the gap in the leaves around his body, a thick red stream of blood trickled, oozing across the floor as it spread into an ugly pool. It touched the bright metal of the pistol and dulled it with red tarnish. It crawled past a broken container and, as if it had met a dam, lapped against the outflung hand of an old, unconscious man.

A man more dead than alive.

CHAPTER NINE

John thought that the shift would never end. He stood at the counter examining an endless line of passengers bound for Earth and tried to keep his mind on what he was doing. It wasn't easy. He had too many other things to worry about and, because of that worry, he'd been losing too much sleep.

Madge had started spending again.

At first he thought that she had learned sense, the shock of realising just how near she was to being bonded had made her stop her extravagances, but only for a while. Now the apartment was getting redolent of the aromas of imported food and costly liquor. Half-used cosmetics littered the place and her dress bill was something he couldn't stand to think about. Worse than that were her continued hints of how he could make some easy money.

He was glad when the shift ended and he could leave the sheds.

Before going home, he had a drink at a nearby tavern, then another and yet another. It was the same place where Phil had first told him about the fixed gambling and he noticed without surprise that the waitress had gone and her place had been taken by a pert brunette. Bonded, he supposed, or dead, and thinking about it filled him with a swift impatience to get home and have it out with his wife.

Phil was waiting for him when he reached the apartment. The smoothly dressed man lounged easily in one of the chairs, a tall drink of imported Scotch in his hand, the smoke of an expensive cigar drifting about his bland features. He nodded as John slammed the door behind him, and Madge looked up with a half-guilty, half-defiant expression from where she sat, dipping into a huge box of chocolates.

"You're late, John," she said. "Been drinking again?"

"What if I have?"

"You might remember that you've a home to come to and a wife waiting for you." She ate another chocolate. "Phil's been waiting almost an hour."

"He probably enjoyed it." John scowled at the chocolates. "What did I tell you about spending, Madge? These things cost over a credit each by the time they've been lifted up from Earth. Damn it! Why the hell don't you do as I say?" Worry sharpened his voice and rage made him pick up the box of sweets and fling them against a wall.

"John! How dare you?"

"How?" He glared at her painted face. "Like this." Cream spattered the floor as his foot smashed the chocolates to ruin. "I'm not warning you again, Madge. If you won't learn, then to hell with you! I'll quit and we'll both be stuck. Then you can work or be bonded and I don't give a damn which you choose."

"You wouldn't dare!" Anger pulled her mouth into a down-curving arc and thick lines from mouth to nose showed through the heavy makeup. "Let me tell you that you'd better be careful what you say to me and how you treat me. I could get you put away for ten years for what you've done and you know it."

"Do it then. Do it and lose your meal ticket."

"Why you..." She looked helplessly at Phil. "Can you understand the man? A fortune in his hands and he begrudges me a few luxuries. I was a fool ever to have married him and a bigger fool to follow him to the Moon."

"Calm down." Phil drew deeply on his cigar.

"But you heard him! Is that any way to treat a lady?"

"Shut up!" Phil stared at her, his cold eyes hard. "You talk too much, Madge. John is right in what he says."

"That's right. Take his side. You're all against me, all of you." Suddenly she was in tears, the sound of her sobs harsh against the silence of the room.

John licked his lips. "Stop it, Madge," he said gently. "I didn't mean to make you cry, but you mustn't spend money like this. We just haven't got it."

"You could get it," she sniffled. "You could get lots of money if you wanted to. And if you loved me, you would."

"What's she talking about?" John stared blankly at the small man. "What's all this about?"

"Can't you guess, John?" Phil stared at the glowing tip of his cigar. "You did it once, you know. Why not twice?"

"No."

"Why not, John?" The small man kept staring at his cigar. "It's so simple. You didn't get into trouble last time, did you? Trust my friend. He can take care of everything, and it will go off as smooth as silk."

"No."

"Be reasonable, John. Why not?"

"Look, Phil," said John tightly. "I won't do it. If for no other reason it is too risky. They've taken to splitting shifts now. No one knows just when he will be on duty. The last time everything almost fell down because of this. I didn't get into the sheds until most of the passengers from that Venusian transport had been cleared. If your man hadn't been both lucky and intelligent he'd have gotten caught for certain. I won't risk it again."

"Because of the variable schedules?"

"Yes."

"That can be avoided, John." Phil looked up from his examination of the cigar. "You get some notice as to what shifts you're on, don't you?"

"Yes. A week. But that's no good, Phil. The shortest transit is three weeks and I can't be certain I'll be on when any particular ship is due."

"Perhaps not, but a week's notice is long enough." Phil put down the cigar and sipped at his Scotch. "A private space yacht, an etherphone message, and the ship could land at exactly the right time. It could be done, John, and it would be the easiest thing imaginable."

"A private space yacht?" John looked stunned. "Man, those things cost millions." He stared at the small man. Are you trying to tell me that these friends of yours are willing to go that far?"

"Why not, John? There's money in it. Lots of money." He smiled and glanced at Madge, now no longer weeping. "Money for all of us."

"No."

"Don't be stubborn, John. I know that you need the money and there's another thing." He looked apologetic. "I hate to say this, but certain people are depending on you. They may not like it if you let them down. They may even drop a hint or two..." He shrugged. "Ten years on Mercury slaving at forced labour is a thing to be avoided, John. Do I make myself clear?"

"Too clear." John didn't trouble to hide his disgust. "So it's blackmail now. If I don't do as you say, you'll see that I suffer for the past favour I did you. If I do as you ask, then I'm in deeper than before. To hell with you!"

"You may as well be hung for a sheep as a lamb, John." Phil drained his glass. "And believe me, if you don't play along, you'll hang."

"Is that a threat?"

"Threat?" The small man smiled. "Shall we call it a promise, John? I prefer the word and," he smiled again, "it's a lot nearer the truth." He rose and moved towards the door. "Think it over. Ten years in jail against a nice thick wad of credits. We'll talk about it tomorrow, yes?"

"Tomorrow." John slumped tiredly into a chair. "Yes, we'll talk about it then."

He never had the chance.

They arrested him as soon as he had checked in at the sheds. Two guards fell in beside him and escorted him to the Superintendent's office. They left him there facing the smooth, bland, super-efficient man behind the desk and John could hear their heavy boots as they went to wait outside.

He stared at the Super. "What's all this about?"

"You were on duty when the Venusian transport, flight 465, landed. Is that right?"

"I don't know." John frowned, knowing that the Super knew that he would remember, and knowing that it would be useless, even dangerous, to deny it. "That's right. That was the time when we operated on split shifts. Why? What of it?"

"Contraband was smuggled through on that trip. I intend to find out how."

"An accident?" John shrugged. "Sometimes someone bound to slip up. Anyway, why tell me?"

"I've been checking the records." The Super took a thin sheaf of correlated film strips from a drawer. "All conversations appear to be satisfactory. No odd remarks or attempts at bribery, collusion, recognition or persuasion other than those accounted for by seized material or convicted smugglers. You caught a man during that shift I believe?"

"Yes. A young fool who should have known better. He tried to smuggle a packet of seeds through disguised as a wrist watch."

"Yes, I remember now. How did you spot him?"

"Casing was too thick and the hands didn't move."

"I see. You are a shrewd inspector, Weston. It seems strange that you could have been so careless."

"How do you mean?"

"The records show that you deliberately ignored the readings of the instruments which showed a large amount of unexplained metal. The scanning eyes show that your inspection of what appeared to be an electronic camera was casual. How do you account for this?"

"I don't." John forced himself to be calm. "I examined the camera and it explained the metal registered on the detectors. There were a few other things, I forget just what, but otherwise the man was clean and I passed him as such."

"I see." The Superintendent nodded, staring down at the record sheets, and John wondered what had made the man examine them so carefully. Normally they were given a routine check over to make certain that the inspectors were doing their job, but he knew that there was nothing on the records to direct suspicion towards him. His explanation was reasonable and would normally have been accepted without question. He fidgeted as he stood before the desk. "Will that be all, sir?"

"No, Weston, it will not." The Super dropped the record sheets. "Let me make myself clear about this. You are not the only man who worked on that shift to be questioned and there will be others after you. You see, Weston, we know for a certainty that a box of contraband was smuggled through during that shift. A box, mark you, a sealed metal box. Obviously one of the inspectors was in collusion with the carrier and passed it through."

"Yes, sir." John tried not to sweat. "Am I to assume that you suspect me?"

"We suspect everyone, but you are the obvious one." The Superintendent leaned back in his chair. "I remember warning you about the state of your finances. I have checked your account and find that just before the period in question your account mended itself with surprising speed." He leaned forward. "Where did you get that money, Weston?"

"From investments. I bought certain articles and sold them again at a small profit." John shrugged. "As you have checked my account, you have probably tracked all the cheques paid in and know that I speak the truth."

"That will come later...if necessary." The Super relaxed as he stared at the man before him. "I may as well be frank with you, Weston. You are the only inspector with a large, unaccounted mass of metal passed through his station. You were, and are, in financial difficulties. I must ask you to submit to the lie detector."

"And if I refuse?"

"If you are innocent, there is no reason for refusal." The Super looked steadily at the man before him. "I could pass every inspector through the detector and, by elimination, you would be the obviously guilty party. I could obtain a court order to force you to submit. Still, that would take time, and we have no time to waste. I ask you, as a man, will you submit to the examination?"

"No."

"I see." The Super seemed disappointed. "I..."

"There is no need," said John calmly. "I am the man you are looking for."

"You admit collusion?"

"Yes."

"I see." For a long moment the Superintendent stared down at his desk. Then, rising to his feet, moved towards a door at the rear of his office. It opened at his touch and a uniformed man passed through. He looked at John.

"Is this the man?"

"Yes." The Super kept his eyes on the ground. "You may use this office. I will give the necessary orders." He left then, walking with dragging feet, and to John, he seemed suddenly tired and very old.

It made him feel sorry. It made him feel ashamed. It made him feel glad that the lies and pretence were over and he felt a warm glow, the reward of honesty to a basically honest man, the emotion which made a criminal confess to his every crime. He had done a terrible thing, he was filled with regret, and now he wanted to make what reparation he could. He stared at the uniformed man, recognising the insignia of a captain of the Trans-World Police.

"I passed the man..." He was interrupted by the captain.

"One moment, if you please." Opening a drawer, the official took out a couple of handgrips and switched on a recorder. "Hold these, please."

"A lie detector?" John shrugged, but grasped the contacts. "I have no intention of lying."

"Perhaps not, but it is well to be sure." The captain made an adjustment to the recorder. "My name is Captain Raymond of the Trans-World Police. I am interviewing John Weston, a customs inspector at Luna Station." He glanced at John. "Is that your name and rank?"

"It is."

"You admit collusion in that you aided a certain person, at present unknown, to smuggle contraband past inspection?"

"I do."

"What was the contraband?"

"I don't know."

"Who was the person?" Raymond kept his eyes on the register of the detector as he asked the questions and John knew that the veracity of his answers was being recorded together with his voice.

"I don't know."

"Did you work alone in this?"

"Yes."

"I will repeat the question. Did you work alone in this?"

"Yes."

"Who was your confederate?"

John dropped the contacts and shook his head. "I'm sorry. I willing to take the punishment for what I did, but mine is the responsibility. I will not answer your question."

"I see." Raymond lifted his eyes from the register and stared at John. He seemed to come to some sudden decision, for he smiled and gestured towards a chair. "Sit down, John. I think it is time someone told you what all this is about."

"Thank you."

"A few hours ago, we received a message from Venus. It was a strange message and caused quite a bit of bother. A man named Merrill, the head of the Hunting Syndicate out there, informed us of a certain box which he said had been smuggled through the station here. This box is probably the most dangerous thing ever to have threatened Humanity. I use his own words, you understand, but we have checked with the biologists and what he says could be true, exaggerated or not, what he told us of the contents of that box makes it imperative for us to find it as soon as possible." He paused. "You understand me, John? We must find that box."

"How can I help you?"

"You say that you don't know who smuggled it through or where it went. I believe you. But at the same time, you must have had a confederate. Someone in the station put you up to this." He looked at John. "I want to know who."

"Sorry. I can't tell you that."

"Can't? Or won't?"

"Won't."

The captain sighed and John was surprised to see little globules of sweat clinging to the man's forehead.

"This is serious, John. I can't tell you how serious, but that box may contain the death of a world. We've got to find it, and find it soon! That confederate of yours may be able to give us an idea of where to look." Anger began to force its way past his control. "Damn it, man! This is no time for misplaced loyalty! You've got to help us."

"He wouldn't know the man." John swallowed as he realised that he had admitted to a confederate. "I saw him. I'll admit to this, but where he went and what he did with the box I wouldn't know.

"Someone knows." Raymond wiped his moist forehead. "That box contains spores, John. Parasitical spores from Venus. You know what can happen if some fool scatters them. The soft fruit industry was almost ruined by a few stray spores released by an amateur gardener who hoped to grow an edible fungus. The tobacco famine was due to a mutated spore brought in by accident. You've heard about those things and you know how important it is that nothing like that slips through the inspection here. Merrill, the man on Venus, has warned us what would happen if that box is ever opened. I'm not trying to frighten you, John, but it may well mean the death of every living thing on Earth."

"The box was smuggled through some time ago now," said John slowly. "It must have been opened by now."

"Perhaps not. We must hope not. Our information leads us to believe that we still have a chance." Raymond clenched his hands in tearing impatience. "But minutes count, seconds, and we're wasting time here. If you know anything, for God's sake, tell us. We've got to find that box!"

"Yes," said John quietly. "I believe you."

"Then you will help us?"

John nodded, not speaking, and silently picked up the two contacts leading to the lie detector.

CHAPTER TEN

Sam couldn't open the box. He glowered down at it as it rested on the small table in the guarded room, and looked up with quick irritation as the guard put his head inside the door.

"Could I help you, sir?"

"No. I'll be out in a moment."

"Yes, sir."

He was suspicious, Sam could tell that, and he swore as he made a final attempt to solve the lock-combination on the sealed box. He had remained too long inside the safety deposit room as it was, and it was time to go. He grunted as the lid refused to open, the smooth metal seeming to be a solid piece, so tight were the joints. Then, reluctantly, he threw it back in the compartment and slammed the door.

Outside, he looked for the man who was following him. It amused him a little, this constant surveillance, and he wondered what Stephan hoped to gain by it. He had left the fat man with the option of finding the money due or losing the box, and so far he hadn't received any money.

He hadn't been able to open the box either.

He frowned as he thought about it. Obviously it was fastened by some form of electronic lock and could only be sprung by someone with knowledge of the correct setting. Stephan must have the combination. Merrill would have given it to him but, until he got the box, he couldn't use it. On the other hand, though Sam had the box, he couldn't open it without the combination, and the thought of a fortune lying so near and yet so far made him sweat.

Irritably he strode down the street, the shadow following, and brooded on how to solve the problem. If he took the box from the vault, the chances were that he'd be robbed within the hour. Stephan was getting as desperate as he was, and the man wouldn't hesitate at using violence. Energy tools would get the box open, but Sam knew enough about mutated seeds to realise that excessive heat or violence could disturb their delicate balance so that, if they grew at all, they wouldn't breed true. The only answer was to cut the box open, and that mean finding a workshop with the right tools, an owner who wouldn't ask questions, and some method of selling the seeds once he had obtained them.

And he was getting short of money.

A turbo-car whined down the street, its engine shrilling as it slowed to take a corner, and Sam jerked back out of the road, cursing the driver for his carelessness. He stiffened as something dug into the small of his back.

"Take it easy," whispered a voice. "If you move or yell, I'll blast your kidneys."

"Stephan?"

"That's right." The gun dug harder. "He wants to see you. Get in the car."

Sam grunted and stepped into the rear compartment of the halted turbo-car. The man who had been following him climbed in beside him, the small, wicked-looking high-velocity pistol in his hand. The door slammed shut and the car streaked off with a shrilling whine from its turbine engine, the acceleration throwing Sam hard against the rear cushions.

"So fatty wants to see me, does he?" He grinned. "I wonder what about?"

"You'll find out."

"You're wasting your time. I haven't got the box."

The man didn't answer, but the gun slammed down with painful force and the hunter swore at the pain from his bruised knee-cap. He sat the rest of the journey in glowering silence.

Stephan looked up from where he sat at a wide desk as Sam was shoved into a small, obviously soundproofed room, in a house about ten miles from the city. The fat man seemed shrunken, as if clawing worry had stripped away some of his flesh and his eyes held a hard brittleness as he stared at the hunter. He jerked his head and the man with the gun left the room.

Sam fumbled for a cigarette. "You wanted to see me?"

"Yes." Stephan leaned forward, one fat hand waving away the drifting clouds of smoke. "You can guess why, Steel. This thing has gone on too long."

"Have you got the money?"

"No."

Sam shrugged. He leaned back in his chair and, pursing his lips, blew a writhing smoke ring towards the glow-light.

The fat man almost snarled with irritation. "Look," he said coldly. "Let's be reasonable about this. I can give you a little money, not much, but we can call it an advance on good faith. The box is useless to you. You haven't got the set-up to either grow the plants or market the drugs and, if you try to find a backer, you're liable to get into trouble. I have the set-up and you have the seeds." He spread hands. "Isn't it only common sense that we get together?"

"As partners?"

"If you wish."

"I wish." Sam grinned. "Now you're talking sense. I'll take money and you can cut me in on what you make." He looked at glowing tip of his cigarette. "A half share, shall we say?"

"No."

"You can't get the box without me," said Sam quietly. "You know that, and you've tried every other way you can think of. Unless I play along, you'll never get the stuff."

"Unless I get it, you won't live to boast about it." Stephan sucked in his lips. "I'm not playing, Steel. I mean what I say and, believe me, you won't die easily. I've too much tied up in this thing to be nice about my methods. Before I'm through with you, you'll be screaming for death as an addict screams for his drugs."

"But you still won't get the box," reminded Sam. He stared at Stephan through a veil of smoke. He knew that the fat man meant everything he said, that he had reached his limit of patience and was ready to cut his losses and take his revenge. It was time to come to an agreement. "You don't scare me," he said calmly. "But I'm a man who can face things in a realistic way. A third share."

"Impossible." Stephan relaxed. "I admire you, Steel, and I'm sure that we'll get along well together, but I can't give you that much. There are others to consider." He hesitated. "I was thinking of offering you a tenth."

"Not enough." Sam crushed out the butt of his cigarette. "I'll earn my money, Stephan, and without the box you couldn't get a credit. Make it a quarter."

"Sorry." There was a grim finality in the fat man's voice. "We're talking about millions, Steel, but there are others to take care of." He looked at his fingernails. "A fifth, and you take charge of the goon squad." He looked at the hunter. "Well?"

Sam shrugged. To insist on more was to get it...together with a knife in the back at the first opportunity. Greed was a self-de- structive attribute and the wise man knew when he'd sucked the sponge dry. Sam was a wise man. "I'll take it." He rose from his chair. "What's the plan?"

"You get the box and bring it back here." Anticipation warmed the fat man's voice. "Better come at night. We'll open the box and start planting right away." He gestured towards the rear of the house. "I've got seed beds prepared and we can force the ini- tial growth. While we're waiting for the harvest, you can contact outlets and arrange for deliveries." He smiled. "Tony can go with you."

"To make sure I deliver? Or to save you a fifth share?" Sam didn't try to hide his suspicions. "No thanks. In a set-up like this we've got to trust each other and the sooner we start, the better." He held out his hand. "I'll take the money now, for expenses, and you'll have the box by midnight. Better let me have the address. I don't want to get lost."

Stephan shrugged but didn't argue. Sam knew that the fat man would have him followed, but he didn't let it worry him. Chances had to be taken in any game where millions were at stake, and he didn't blame the fat man for taking elementary precautions.

The turbo-car dropped him in the centre of the city and he waited until he had spotted his shadow. The next hour he spent in shaking the man off, spotting a second trailer in the process. When he was certain that he had lost both, he relaxed over a meal and a bottle of Martian wine. From the restaurant, he went to a local protection office and gave careful instructions, paying out a thick wad of money and making sure that the hired guards understood just what he wanted them to do. Not until almost midnight did he enter the depository and he smiled as he spotted the two men lounging across the street. The shadows had picked up his trail again.

At the safe deposit, he recovered the box, took one other precaution, and caught a jetcopter from the landing stage on the roof.

He arrived back at the house a few minutes after midnight and grinned at the relieved expression on the fat man's hard features.

"Worried?" Sam set the box down on the table. "You needn't be, but just in case you get any smart ideas, let me warn you that I'm not quite a fool. Kill me if you like, but I promise that you won't live long enough to regret it."

"What do you mean?"

"Nothing." Sam pushed the box towards the fat man. "Just talking."

Stephan looked at him, his eyes hard with suspicion. Then, as he rested his hands on the smooth metal of the box, he shrugged. "I'm not going to kill you, Steel. You can be too valuable." He stared down at the box. "At last," he whispered. "I've got it at last."

"Aren't you going to open it?" Sam glanced at his wrist chronometer. "I don't want to hang about here all night."

"There's no hurry." Stephan picked up the box and walked towards the door.

Sam strode after him. "Where are you going?"

"To the laboratory. There is some equipment there I may need." Stephan led the way into a wide glass-walled room. Windows lined one wall and, by the dim light of the Moon, Sam could see the ranked hothouses and hydroponic beds of a small but compact experimental plant station. He stood by the windows for a moment, staring out into the darkness, and turning so that the light fell full on his face. Then he walked to where the fat man had sat down at a bench, the box resting before him.

"Hurry up and open it," snapped Sam impatiently. "I'm curious to know what's inside."

"I told you what's inside. Seeds."

"Maybe, but I'm still curious. After all I did fetch that thing all the way from Venus."

"That's right." Stephan seemed amused. "Sit down, Steel, and let's have a look at what you carried." He rested his hands on the smooth metal. "Clever things, these electronic locks. No one can possibly open one without the combination, they can't be forced and they can't be tripped like an ordinary lock." His fingers drifted over the container. "In effect, this is a solid piece of metal, the static charge is holding the lid down by molecular cohesion, thus making a perfect seal. To bleed the static charge, it is essential to know both the setting and the activating charge. Without those, the box cannot be opened."

"I know of a way." Sam tried not to yawn. "Cut it open."

"Force would, of course, open it," admitted Stephan. "And force would no doubt be used if necessary." He looked at the hunter. "Fortunately it isn't necessary."

His thick fingers hesitated at the smooth seam and his breath rasped in his throat as he spun the tiny setting wheel. "Twenty, eighteen, one, four, two, nine, seven." He grunted as he reached for a double-pronged electrical contact. "Now the activating charge and the lid will spring open. Five microvolts at two milliamps." He adjusted the controls. "Now."

He moved the prong towards the box.

CHAPTER ELEVEN

High above the city, a jetcopter droned through the night as it swung in a complex pattern over the Earth below. Instruments littered the cabin, leaving little room for the crew, and John winced as he tried to ease his cramped legs. Captain Raymond glanced towards him, then back at a man crouched over a radio-like instrument.

"Any luck?"

"Getting a signal, captain. I'm waiting to hear from the others so as to locate the source."

"Can they find the box with that?" John looked at the tracing equipment and Raymond shrugged.

"I don't know. They use them on Venus to track down marked game and Merrill said the box was contaminated with one of the commercial radioactives used in hunting. The trouble is that the stuff would have worn off by now, but we may be lucky." He stared at John. "Comfortable?"

"No complaints." The inspector swallowed. "What I can't understand is why you brought me along with you at all. I should be in jail by now."

"You'll get there," promised Raymond grimly. "But we need you. Aside from that other man—Phil, you called him—you are the only man to have seen the carrier. We could build up a mental picture of your memories, but we haven't the time. You're here to identify him." He looked at the tracer operator. "Got it yet?"

"Yes, sir. It's in the city right enough. Business section."

"Sure?"

"Yes, sir. We're pinpointing it now."

"Right." Raymond leaned forward and touched a man on the shoulder. "Order the seeding to start at once." He shrugged at John's questioning expression. "It's going to create hell with the weather forecast, but we daren't take a chance. Rain will help to wash the air and ground the spores, so I've ordered seeding with dry ice to force an artificial rain over the city area." He pointed to where the thin trails of rocket planes lifted towards the sky. "There they go."

"Have you found the box?" John didn't look at the captain.

"I hope so. That man Phil told us that the carrier landed at Glynod and we trailed him from there. Merrill, too, told us he thought that the Earth contact was in this hemisphere and most likely in this area. Something to do with the population figures and winds. Anyway, we've used the tracer over the entire continent and this is the first lead." Raymond thinned his lips. "We're lucky that the commercial element they use on Venus isn't used here at all. Otherwise the thing would be hopeless." He grunted as the jetcopter dipped and began to drift downwards. "Got it?"

"Yes, sir." The tracer man removed his earphone and rubbed his ears. "Down in that building." He looked at his map. "It's a safe deposit building and we can land on the roof stage."

"It makes sense." Raymond pursed his lips. "A safe deposit box would be the safest place he could leave it unless he made immediate delivery." He frowned. "I wonder why he didn't hand it straight over? Still, it's lucky for us he didn't." He swore as the machine bounced to a bad landing.

The manager was apologetic but firm. Sorry, but this was a private depository and he just couldn't open all the boxes.

Raymond swore with tearing impatience and almost shook the little man. "This is an emergency, you fool! I'm with the Trans-World Police and I tell you that we've got to search those boxes."

"No." The manager was defiant. "I can't allow that."

"We could get a court order to force your cooperation."

"Then get it." The little man smiled as he looked at the captain. "Until then, no."

"Wait a minute." John thrust himself forward. "We don't want to open every box. Just one. You will let us examine one of the boxes?"

"I'm sorry, but..."

"We believe that there's a bomb in that box," snapped Raymond. "Unless you cooperate, it may blow up the entire building. Is that what you want?"

"No." The little man looked worried. "Of course not. Which box is it you wish to examine?"

"Show him." Raymond turned to the tracer man. "Pick it out and get moving."

"Sorry, sir, but I can't." The operator looked apologetic. "The instruments aren't fine enough and there is too much interference for me to pinpoint a single vault. It was hard enough to locate the building itself."

"Damn!" Raymond bit his lip. "Wait! You take photographs of all your customers?"

"Naturally. For identification purposes in case they lose their key or forget their name." He smiled knowingly at the captain. "It has happened before, you know, and we like to keep a record."

"Get them." Raymond stared at John. "Now's the chance for you to do something helpful. You've seen the carrier and I want you to pick him out of the files. Can you do that?"

John nodded and, taking the stack of cards from the manager, began to skim through them.

"Here he is." He held out a photograph card.

The manager took it and read off the number. "X11354. The "X" means that his box is an electronic one." He nodded. "I remember the gentleman. He was in a short while ago."

"Was he?" Raymond caught the man by the arm. "Quick! Get that box open."

"I shall have to get the master pattern," objected the manager. We keep it in the vault."

"Then get it. But hurry, that bomb may go off at any moment." The captain grinned as the manager hurried away, then abruptly became serious. He jerked his head at a guard. "You! Take us to box X11354."

The manager met them in the small cubicle-lined room. He was nervous and, as he pressed the master pattern to the sensitised plate, seemed almost to tremble. He gave a gasp as the drawer slid open, then looked reproachfully at the captain. "Why, it's empty!"

"Empty!" Raymond jerked the little man out of the way. "Damn!" He grunted as he lifted a sheet of paper from the bottom of the box. "What's this?"

"Read it." John stared over the uniformed man's shoulder and stared at the single sheet half-covered with neat writing. "It's a letter from the carrier. I wonder why he left it?"

"To whom it may concern," read out the captain. "If this is found it will mean that I am dead. The man responsible for my murder is known as Stephan, a trader in illicit narcotics from Venus, and is to be found at the following address." Raymond stared at the tense faces circling him. "Damn! We're too late. Steel must have taken the box to deliver it to his contact." He glared at the radio operator. "Quick! Alert all patrols to..." He snapped the address. "Wide coverage and full air curtain. Hurry!"

John clutched the captain's arm as they ran upstairs towards the landing stage. "What's it all about? Why should Steel leave a note?"

"He didn't trust his partner in crime and left the note as a form of insurance. He knew the box would be opened and cleared after his rental expired and left the address as a clue." Raymond swore as he tripped and almost fell. "The radioactives on the box contaminated the drawer, that's how we found it, but Steel beat us to it by minutes."

"Can't we trace the box now?"

"No. The tracer element has worn out. Those things have a short half-life, but we know where he took the box, so it doesn't matter." He swore again as he stumbled onto the roof. "Damn it! They're probably opening the box this very minute." He jumped into the jetcopter and rapped swift orders to the pilot. "You heard the message?"

"Yes, sir."

"Good. Then get us there at top speed." He wiped beads of sweat from his forehead as the machine almost sprang into the air.

It wasn't far but, to John, it seemed as if the journey would never end. To Raymond, it was a nightmare. He kept seeing the gushing cloud of released spores as the box was opened, a thin, almost invisible cloud settling on human flesh, springing into terrible fecundity, sporing and spreading all over the planet. He shook his head as a shatter of rain struck against the transparent hood of the cabin.

"At last! The clouds must be thin up there." He hunched forward as droning reports came in over the radio.

"Area blocked and ground cordon in place. Air coverage assembled."

"On target, sir." The pilot stabbed his thumb downwards. "That's the place."

"Right." Raymond peered down through the rain curtain. "I hope they haven't heard us. Dump the gas."

"It won't do much good in this rain, sir," said the pilot dubiously. "The wind is all wrong, too. It will blow it away before it could be effective."

"Dump it anyway, then settle." Raymond leaned forward as the machine bucked as a stream of small anaesthetic gas bombs fell towards the ground below. He swore as he saw the thin white streamers being blown away by the wind and flattened by the rain. "You were right. The damn gas is useless." He pulled a gun from his belt and checked the loading. "Set down. I'm going in there."

"What about lights, sir?"

"Order the other 'copters to switch on their searchlights and cover the house and grounds. Hurry, now. Set me down."

The machine tilted, veered a little as the rising wind caught it, then drifted towards the dark ground below. Lights blazed around him as the other jetcopters settled and drifted a hundred feet above the ground, their search beams set at wide aperture and dispersed focus.

Raymond waited until the wheels touched down then jerked open the cabin door and jumped outside. Air blasted around him from the spinning rotors of the ship, and his nostrils stung with the taint of gas. He crouched, the pistol levelled in his hand, then made a rush towards the back of the building.

Fire winked at him from behind the angle of a wall and glass shattered from the hothouses ranked all around. He ducked, rolled, sent a stream of slugs towards the unseen marksman and blinked as they exploded into incandescence against the wall.

Cautiously he crept forward, cursing the lights above, for not only did they show him the grounds, but they betrayed his position to the enemy. Again, fire winked at him, this time from a different position, and he yelled as he caught a glimpse of a familiar uniform.

"You there! Protection Officer! Stop your fire! This is the police!" He waited a moment, then waved his arm so that the marksman could see the braid on his sleeve.

"Sorry." The protection officer stepped from behind cover. "We were ordered to protect our client against any danger. He didn't tell us to expect the police."

"Who else did you think would use jetcopters?" Raymond scowled at the man. "Where is your client?"

"I don't know. There was a little trouble in the house, some shooting and a lot of yelling. It wasn't our client; he showed himself just afterwards, so we didn't go in. When you landed, we asked him what to do and he said to beat you off. Naturally we didn't guess that you were the police."

"It's about time you private armies were stopped." Raymond brushed dirt from his knee. "Cover me. I'm going inside."

"Alone?"

"No. You're coming with me, and you have full authority to kill anything which moves." Tensely he strode towards the silent house.

The back door was locked, but a stream of slugs from a high-velocity pistol blew it open. Inside, Raymond stared at a glass-walled laboratory, a mess of electrical and botanical equipment and at a dead man lying on the floor. He stooped over the body, grunting as he rolled the inert figure onto its back and stared down at the hard, fat features.

"This might be Stephan," he muttered. "But where the hell is Steel? And where is the box?"

"There's someone at the front of the house," whispered the protection officer. "I heard a groan. It could have been a groan. Sounded like it, anyway."

They found Sam in the front room, the box between his knees, one hand gripping his stomach and the other holding a pistol. Blood made an ugly pool in which he sat. Two huddled figures had stained the wall with red. He swore when he heard them, blood trickling from his bitten lips, and the gun in his hand sent its spiteful cracks echoing through the building. Raymond ducked. Heat seared his cheek from exploding bullets.

"Steel! This is the Trans-World Police! You're under arrest!"

"Am I?" Blood-choked laughter mingled with the report of the gun. "Come and get me then."

"Listen, Steel." Raymond tried to keep the desperation out of his voice. "That box, the one you're holding, don't open it."

"Why not?" The gun fell silent. They could hear soft sounds as if a man were trying to move without legs. "Police, eh? What do you want me for?"

"Smuggling."

"That all?" Sam coughed and red fluid gushed from his mouth. "Come on in, then. I won't shoot; gun's empty anyway. And I don't want to die alone."

He grinned up at them as they knelt beside him. "That fat swine Stephan did this. Crossed me. Had hidden guards watching me. I didn't know." He coughed again. "I played him along. He had the combination and I didn't, but the fat fool told me what activating charge to use, so I let him have it and took the box."

"You killed him?"

"That's right." Sam grinned down at the smooth, bloodstained metal of the sealed container. "All she needs now is five microvolts at two milliamps and she will pop open like a dream."

He winced from the pain of his ripped insides. "Lucky at that. They had old-fashioned pistols, not high-velocity, but more painful this way." His eyes closed and he dragged them open with a supreme effort. "Fatty shouldn't have tempted me the way he did. He would have killed me, I knew that, so I hired some guards." He chuckled. "Hired them with his money. Then he told me the activating charge. He was a fool to have done that."

"You killed him for the box?"

"Why not? Millions in it. Billions. Why take a fifth or a knife in the back when I could have it all?" Sam's eyes closed and his voice began to fade as he whispered over the blood rilling from his mouth. "Millions. A fortune. Chance of a lifetime. Won..."

"He's dead." The protection officer rose to his feet. "Nothing more I can do now."

"No," agreed Raymond. He squatted down beside the dead man and, after everyone else had left, carefully picked up the metal box and stared down at its smooth surface. It looked so harmless, so innocent, but, as he remembered Merrill's dying message, he felt a quick repulsion. Abruptly he twisted the combination dial, relocking the box against all accident, and slowly rose to his feet.

In a way it was almost ironic. Man's greed had endangered the world...and Man's greed had saved it. If Sam hadn't grabbed at the "big chance," if he hadn't wanted the whole instead of the part, then the box would have been opened and nothing could have saved the human race from utter extinction.

Greed. Raymond shook his head as he thought about it. It had led a man to betray his trust. It had caused an old man's death. It had threatened the world, but Man's greatest weakness had, at the same time, proved his one salvation.

Slowly he walked back to the waiting jetcopter.

www.ingramcontent.com/pod-product-compliance
Lightning Source LLC
Chambersburg PA
CBHW011437170626
46808CB00009B/3089